WISER THAN BUTTERFLIES

ADALCITA D. SAN AGUSTIN

ISBN: 0996004904
ISBN-13: 978-0-9960049-09

This book is dedicated to my sister and friend,
Onz

FROM THE AUTHOR

To all my family,

And to all those with whom I humbly share a special kinship,

I thank you for the honor and the privilege.

I bid you peace.

To Kay,
I thank you for the wonderful memorable fellowship we have and my heart leaps with joy and anticipation for opportunities for more treasurable times spent sharing our life's experiences. Life is for loving, laughing, and living.

your friend,
Cita
(Adalcita)

P.S. Give Roy a hug for me.

CHAPTER 1 WHAT'S IN MY HEART

HEART WHISPERS

An unmoving heap quietly hides underneath a tattered blanket on the seat behind the driver. The rusty, dusty car with splash guards covered in dried mud creeps into a gas station at the edge of a rustic town. The car stops before one of twin pumps. Before long, two bearded men emerge with hair disheveled, unkempt clothes, and dirt adorned boots. One of the men sniffs under his arm and reacts, reflexively turning his face away from the danger. Nearby, two elderly women eye the men and keep their distance as they retreat to their vehicle. The taller man reaches for the nozzle of the gas pump and the other, brawnier one, comes up behind him, claps him on the shoulder, and mumbles a few words. Excitedly, the taller one replies,

"You do me great honor, sir." He grins broadly at his driving companion.
"Anything for you, my good friend!" replies the other. "We should celebrate. You deserve it!" he adds as he walks towards the building.
As the taller man wipes a smudge on the window, he hollers over his shoulder, "Shall we get more than one? Aaron will be there."
"One will do," replies the shorter of the two.
"But, last time, he drank more than the two of us did." They both

laugh.
“We’ll ask him to bring some, then. He’s got loads of money,” says the brawny man. As he pauses at the stands, he hollers, “Hey, I'm getting one of these.” He searches his pockets.
“Look here,” the taller one offers, as he approaches with a palmful of coins, “Do you need change?” They eye the headline through the glass.

'FESTIVAL at the FAIRGROUNDS'

Grinning with anticipation, they enter the double doors. As the brawnier one strides down the liquor aisle, the taller of the two approaches the young clerk. He bends down a little and rests his elbow on the counter as he leans forward, beckoning the clerk to do the same. He looks from side to side. Then, in a low serious voice, asks, “We’ve got the money. Have you got the stuff?”
Smiling, the clerk replies pleasantly, “So sorry, but I have no idea as to...”
Straightening now to his full formidable height, the man squints and, under his breath, demands, “Aren’t you Lance?”
The clerk politely explains, “Lance switched schedules with me. Perhaps I can txt him to ask?”
“No, don’t txt him. There’s no need to txt,” the man replies hurriedly, looking over his shoulder.

Just then, the brawny man comes near and places a six-pack of beer on the counter. As he draws his wallet out, the other, taller man leans towards him and loudly whispers, agitated, “This guy doesn’t have it, but now he knows all about us coming and asking for it. What are we going to do now?”

The clerk nervously takes a half step backwards from the counter. The brawnier man very calmly replies, “Nothing. We are doing nothing. This gentleman here will sell us this beer and we shall leave without incident." He looks straight ahead towards the clerk. "Go to the car, Jonathan," he adds, slowly enunciating his words.

With a quick glance at the clerk, Jonathan replies, alarmed, "Do you realize that you've just given away my name? Next thing you know, you'll be politely shaking his hand and introducing yourself," he scoffs, and with that, he turns abruptly on his heels and leaves.

"Don't mind my sidekick there," the other man gestures towards the door. Then more pleasantly, he adds, "By the way, I'm Henry," as he reaches a friendly hand across the counter. "Pleased to meet you." The clerk reluctantly accepts the handshake. Still shaking the clerk's hand, Henry says, "Please tell Lance when you see him, that we came by to pick up some beer." Then Henry nods slowly until the clerk nods back, and he smiles reassuringly, "Relax, Lance will explain." As Henry exits, he holds the door open for a young woman entering with a double-wide stroller.

PACIFIST

Henry walks to the back of the car and stows the beer in the crowded trunk right next to another full six-pack, only the carton of this one looks weathered. Both climb into the car and they drive off with Henry at the wheel. Jonathan looks at his watch, and says, "This is good. We're on schedule. Today's too important for us to be late. I just sent a message."

"Why the hell do you do that?" Henry blurts out.
"Do what?"
"You know what I mean!"
"It's T—E—R—O—C—I,...Triggering Emotive Responses in Otherwise Calm Individuals."
"What?"
"I'm just honing my skills."
"You're full of shit! You made that up," Henry retorts.
"...made that up," Jonathan says, a fraction of a second behind.
"Stop it, Jonathan!" Henry says, eyes narrowing.
"Stop it, Jonathan!" Jonathan says, almost in unison.
"Now, you're asking for it!" says Henry, through gritted teeth.
"...you're asking for it!" Jonathan says almost at the same time, but this time, mimicking Henry's threatening tone.
Slowly, Jonathan grins, pleased with himself. Then suddenly

Henry tries to nudge Jonathan in the head, but Jonathan grabs his wrist. Henry pulls his hand back, disgusted. Snickering now, Jonathan says pompously, "You're so predictable!"

"You know you could've gotten us shot! There is no need to scare the guy shitless just so you could practice your D—E—R on him."
"No, I said T—E—R, Triggering Emotive Responses. And I *didn't* say I was practicing on *him*."

Quickly, Henry grabs his hat from the dash and feins two blows to the head which Jonathan deftly blocks, first with one hand, then the other, without even turning towards Henry. But then Henry strikes him in the gut and the blow lands, sending Jonathan into fits of coughing.

"Predictable? Who did you say was predictable?"
"Hey! No fair," Jonathan exclaims between coughs. "You know I never hit you," he says, now chortling as he recovers.

"There's nothing that says you can't *try* to hit me," Henry taunts him.
"I'm a pacifist. I prefer resolving conflicts through diplomatic means." Jonathan grins and leans away from him in case Henry decides to hit him again.
Henry rolls his eyes. "The stuff you come up with! Seriously! Hang on." Then he whispers, "We're here."

SECRET

As Henry drives the car around the bend, a brick building appears. Slowly he pulls up, turns the engine off, and they coast a good distance in silence before coming to a halt behind a hedge just tall enough to hide the car. They leave the car doors open so as not to let noise give away their plan and inch over stealthily, intent on a mission. Over their shoulders, an innocent butterfly daintily explores a flower as a crow caws menacingly overhead. Meanwhile, the two men scan the schoolyard full of squealing girls.

"There!" they exclaim under their breath simultaneously.
"I saw her first," cries Henry.
"Okay, it's your turn," Jonathan whispers in reply.

With Jonathan right behind, Henry slinks over to where the little girl is sitting on a bench, reading a book, away from the others. He hides behind a tree nearby and then rushes up to her and quickly covers her eyes with his hand.

She gasps, "Oh!" and reflexively puts both of her little hands over Henry's.

Jonathan, who followed close behind, brings his face over her shoulder, close to her ear and whispers, "Guess who?"

The little girl runs her fingers over Henry's skin, but before anyone notices, cries, "Henry!" And she suddenly turns to give him a hug. They both laugh just as Jonathan appears from behind Henry. "Pappy!" she squeals and gives Jonathan a hug too.

"You guess right every time! How do you do that, Moriah?"

"It's a secret," she boasts, skipping towards the car.

She hops into the back seat and the boys climb into their usual seats, with Jonathan at the wheel. Moriah's toys and books hang out from the back pocket of Henry's seat where she can easily reach them. Moriah and her faithful escorts wave warmly to an elderly couple returning to their vehicle with their grandchild as they drive by, excited.

INFLUENCE

Meanwhile at a modest house in town, Marion and her very good friend Mrs. Pingrey decorate a cake.

"Jonathan just sent word that they're on their way. Henry's promptness is rubbing off on him," says Mrs. Pingrey as she puts down her phone.

Marion licks icing off her fingers. "For the most part Henry's a good example. He shows such responsibility and maturity for one his age."

"Yes, indeed, you wouldn't think that being born the calendar year before Jonathan would have such a great impact. Henry carries on as if he is much older."

"But, Henry's choices lately, the drinking, and the cussing. I'm not certain I want anything else to rub off onto Jonathan."

"Do not worry, Marion. I think Jonathan is more his own person than he appears to be. And I've only ever heard him use cuss words under anesthesia." They laugh at the memory. "If anything, Marion, it is Henry who needs to watch out for Jonathan's influence. One can see, you've raised 'm well."

"I'm just waiting for the day he'll act his age."

“Well, ever since he got Moriah, he has had to set aside childhood things. I think he’s just trying to stretch it out a bit. And besides, he just got a promotion.”

“He can be responsible when he wants to be. I just wish Edmund were here to help him find a sense of direction. It’s like,” she searches for a word, “he’s floating.”

“Seems to me, his purpose right now is to be a good father to his little girl, and he’s doing just that.”

“I've got to admit, he has taken his promise to heart.”

Just then Mrs. Pingrey notices the clock. “Come on! They’ll be here any minute!”

They finish decorating in the nick of time. “Thanks for your help, Mrs. Pingrey.”

“Glad to do it, Marion.” Mrs. Pingrey leaves through the kitchen door to freshen up at her house next door. She hurriedly crosses the two adjoining yards, an expansive lawn bordered by an extensive array of vegetables, herbs, and nectar-rich flowers.

REPARTEE

Soon after Mrs. Pingrey leaves, Jonathan, Henry, and Moriah arrive and enter through the mudroom. Jonathan eyes the clock. They have about an hour before the house is teaming with soon-to-be-over-sugared little children, each toting their own set of brave guardians. Moriah dumps all of her stuff on the floor at Henry's feet then runs off to the dining room for a kiss from her Nanna. “Happy Birthday, sweetheart. Now hurry! They're almost here!” Marion sends her upstairs to bathe and change.

Jonathan removes his mud caked boots while Henry picks up after Moriah. As he puts everything away, Jonathan exclaims, “She's got you trained well, doesn't she!”

“We've been in your house all of twenty seconds. How is it you do that, get on father mode and get all defensive of Moriah in such short order?”

“We've talked about this before. How's she supposed to learn, if you do that?”

“She knows not to pull it on anyone else, just me,” Henry gloats, rather proudly, as if Moriah's behavior is a product of intent.

Marion pokes her head into the mudroom. “Everything go well on your trip?" She grabs an armful of towels and table linen from the top of the dryer.

Jonathan, now standing, gives her a quick kiss. "Hello, Mother."

Henry looks up. "We'll tell you all about it after the party," he says as he struggles with his other boot.

Not wanting to let the issue go, Jonathan turns to him. "You're spoiling her."

"Yes, I am." Henry grins at Marion as he stands. She smiles back, amused at their repartee.

"I can't get through to him." Jonathan throws his hands up. "I'm going to get cleaned up." And he leaves the mudroom exasperated.

She offers Henry a towel. "You can wash up in the guest bath to save yourself a trip home."

Henry suavely puts his arms around Marion's waist, stack of laundry still between them, and leans back, as if admiring her. "Mrs. Brookes, you do know you're the loveliest lady in the world, don't you?" And he promptly plants a kiss on her cheek.

Marion starts to laugh, but suddenly, Jonathan pokes his head back in the doorway and admonishes Henry, "Get your hands off, and stop fooling around! We've got work to do." Then he turns to Marion with penetrating eyes. "You know he's just trying to get on your sweet side!"

She dismisses him with a laugh, then hurriedly adds, "Get on, you two! How are we supposed to get ready in time? I still need chairs in the garden!"

ANTICIPATION

The scruffy, smelly, suspicious-types transform nicely after washing up. From underneath the scary dirt emerge unforgivably handsome young men, now looking much younger after a proper shave. Jonathan jaunts down the stairs sporting an unassumingly immaculate countenance. He is tall like a knight, but lanky, like a knight in the making. His biggest advantage, a broad grin that could disarm a dragon.

From the guest room near the stairs, Henry appears. His tanned seasoned freckles still brandish some boyish charm, but something deep in his eyes whispers of a sleeping strength, like that of an ancient castle that had put out its candles for an unburdened slumber. As he rounds the bend, Marion hands him a large dilapidated carton, and they both turn their heads as Aaron's truck rolls up behind the house.

Aaron enters and fills the kitchen doorway with his horseman's frame. But contrary to what his kingly stature would suggest, his presence exudes a calming protective gentleness. He kneels before Moriah, all of angel and delight in the birthday dress Marion meticulously made, and he presents his gift to her with a slight bow, "Happy Birthday, Princess." Moriah curtsies and giggles excitedly, thanks him with a hug, then turns to exchange the box for a birthday tiara which Mrs. Pingrey helps her don. Marion and Mrs. Pingrey then warmly greet Aaron with a hug.

In the kitchen, Henry looks up from the box of stringed lights that were somehow overlooked in the preparations, and greets Aaron with a handshake. A little exasperated he confesses, "I really don't see it, but she insists. She says it's for the ambiance."

Aaron chuckles. "Let me help you, so it won't be too painful. In fact, I'd be glad to do it for you."

Meanwhile, Jonathan approaches Aaron with great anticipation for an especially enthusiastic greeting.

"Congratulations on your promotion, Jonathan! Well done and well deserved!" Aaron gives Jonathan a hefty one-armed hug over a vigorous handshake.

"Thank you, Doctor," Jonathan replies with a big smile. "I am extremely pleased you approve."

"Approve? At the very least!" Aaron puts an arm over Jonathan's shoulder and says, "If your father were here, I think he would say, 'Son, I'm very proud.'" And he gives Jonathan's shoulder a fond shake. Jonathan found himself very pleased at having heard those particular words.

Henry whispers to Aaron, "We'll have a proper celebration after Moriah's party."

"Yeah," Jonathan adds, "Henry got the good beer."

Aaron looks to see Marion isn't near, then says in a low voice, "This is a special occasion. It calls for something better than the best beer."

The boys glance over their shoulder, then look at each other and start laughing, and Aaron joins them. "There's nothing like anticipation to make a party really enjoyable," Henry adds.

Finally, the highlight of the evening. Jonathan announces, "It's time for cake!" and the children all scurry excitedly over to the table in the garden. Suddenly he remembers, ducks into the kitchen and emerges, balancing in his arms a big glass punch dispenser. Aaron offers to help.

"It's alright. I've got it, Doctor," Jonathan says as he carries it out the French doors towards the garden.

"Why does he still do that?" Aaron asks Marion, a little disappointed.

"Call you 'Doctor'?" she says, hunched over the cake, intently trying to get the lighter to work.

"Mmhm," Aaron affirms.

"He chooses to because he respects you. It's a good thing, Aaron. Let him. He needs someone to respect." When all the candles are lit, she picks up the cake gingerly. "Want cake?" she consoles him with a bribe as she walks out towards the garden.

"I really shouldn't," he mutters, only half believing himself, as he arms himself with a serving spatula before diving right behind her out into the melee.

HOW I FEEL

A little later as the guests sing and clap, Jonathan inches over to Marion as she attends to the cake table. He helps her take dishes away to the sink. "Mum, You're okay with me being vocal about my feelings, right?" They return to the table outside.

"I encourage it," Marion says.

"You won't mind me saying it then. What Henry said to you earlier, I don't like it." To avoid her gaze, he keeps his eyes forward towards the guests, and every now and then grins at them, pretending not to be in serious conversation with his mother.

"Oh, Jonathan. Don't be jealous. It's not any different from you saying to me that 'I'm your special someone.'"

"It is so *not* the same! Henry says it, word for word, the way father used to say it to you before he..." He pauses having difficulty finishing his thought. Jonathan can't seem to say these words even after three years.

Her voice softens as one's voice often does when one's heart softens. "You mean before your father died?"

Jonathan looks away. “Well, Henry's *not* father!”

“I'm glad you've told me what's in your heart.” She moves near him, takes a hand to turn his gaze towards her. “Now, let me tell you what's in mine.” Unfortunately, a guest approaches and their conversation is interrupted.

As laughter and music clasp hands and dance in the air, Jonathan runs across the yard with the ball and a gaggle of children at his heels. Henry decides to level the playing field and raises the garden hose, sending Jonathan into the grass whereupon they scramble over him like puppies, Moriah taking lead. There is an air of contentment and coziness as if the house itself took pleasure in holding to its bosom, the delight and merriment of all who are held captive by the starlight that had descended from the heavens and rested at its feet. As the sweet noise plays in its belly, a warmth fills its walls rising all throughout, lulling it with savory reassurance.

Before long, the defenseless cake is besieged and ravaged. Crumbs, proof of the desolation. Aaron's sleeves are rolled halfway up his arms, and wrapped around his growing middle, a strawberry printed towel, his only shield in the battle zone. But now with great anticipation, his eyes are on Moriah's angelic face as she opens his present for her. He is assured that he chose well when she shrieks with surprise and whips her tiny arms around his neck. For a brief moment he savors it all, the echo of her voice, the music, everyone's laughter, brewed with the essence of jasmine in Moriah's delicate hair as it brushes against his cheek as they hug. “So this is how happiness intoxicates!” he mutters to himself.

After the last of the guests have said goodbye, Marion and Mrs. Pingrey enjoy quiet conversation over a cup of tea in the anteroom, while Moriah plays with her new toys. Marion doesn't notice that the gentlemen are not nearly as loud or animated as they are apt to be. But Mrs. Pingrey notices, a skill she acquired over the years, and she files it in her mind as 'notably unusual but not requiring immediate action.' For now, she is content that all is well.

Meanwhile, in the den across the hall, Aaron and the boys have their "beer" in Jonathan's honor.

Aaron, pouring amber liquid into glasses, says softly, "Just a little, you boys have to drive in a bit. We can have more when you come to the ranch tomorrow."

"Shall we close the door?"

"No, no. That will raise suspicion," Aaron warns. They chuckle, and raise their glasses.

"Cheers," they all whisper. Aaron and Henry promptly raise their glasses to their lips and pretend to begin to drink as Jonathan tilts his head back and spills the drink into his throat all at once and swallows.

Aaron and Henry grin at each other and wait. "Congratulations again, Jonathan."

"Yeah, you earned it," they mutter, while eyeing him with

anticipation.

“Thanks. Good stuff. I like it!”

“'I like it!' That's what you say when you eat cake!” Henry retorts, “You've had this before!”

“Nope! First time,” Jonathan boasts.

“Then how...” Henry's eyes narrow.

“He's up to something,” Aaron suggests, throwing Henry a sideways glance.

“Aren't I always?” Jonathan chuckles, amused at their reaction, then adds, “You guys should see your faces.” He chuckles some more just to rub it in and holds out his glass for more.

MY WORD

Later that night after Aaron has gone home, Henry and Jonathan tell Marion they are going to hang out at Henry's place. While Jonathan is talking to Moriah, Marion sees Henry to the car.

"Henry!" she calls out after him, "Wait."

He waves to her with the hand that is toting the other, more worn six-pack of beer. And as Marion approaches, Henry quickly adjusts the blanket to fully cover the stuff on the back seat. She pokes her head in the car window, gives Henry a kiss on the face, and says, "Here, more cake. Thank you."

"For what?"

"Oh, nothing. Maybe, everything." She looks at him adoringly.

"Well, that's rather vague!" He grins.

"Get out of here!" She pushes the side of his head and turns towards the house.

Henry starts counting, "One thousand one, one thousand two, one thousand …."

Before she gets to the door, she turns to him and yells, "Watch out for him!"

"I will," Henry replies, then stops counting and grins.

Just before leaving with Henry, Jonathan says goodbye to Moriah in the dining room.

"Nanna or Mrs. Pingrey will have to read you a story tonight. I can't. I'm sorry. There's something important I have to do. One more birthday hug." They hug. "Make sure you tell them both you love them before you fall asleep, alright?"

"I didn't get a hug from Henry." She looks forlornly outside the window towards the car.

"We're running awfully late as it is. Here, I'll give you a hug for him and I'll give him a hug for you."

"Promise?"

"On my honor!"

Moriah squints, holds Jonathan's face between her hands. "Look me in the eye, please. Do you promise?" Moriah uses a very stern voice.

"Yes, I do!" Jonathan grins proudly, impressed with her best serious-face-imitation to date.

Jonathan reaches the doorway just as Marion nudges Henry's head and laughs. He could tell Henry is grinning. Jonathan eyes Marion as she approaches, then he says hurriedly, "G'night,

Mum. Don't wait up."

She reminds him, "If you can't get home, just stay over at Henry's. And I'll see you tomorrow."

"Stay over at Henry's," he says in chorus. "I know, Mum. Thanks for watching Moriah while I'm gone. Someday soon I'll make it up to you."

"Yes, yes." She gives him a kiss, then she whispers, "I know he's older, but you watch out for him."

"Mum! It's just a beer!" he whines, under his breath so Henry won't hear.

"I counted six," she replies with a smile, "besides what you've both had already!"

As they drive away, Jonathan asks, "Did she see anything?"

"No," Henry replies.

Back at the house, Marion says to Mrs. Pingrey. "My word, that's four times already this week."

"It's alright, it's just a game and a beer. They can't get into too much trouble, can they?" she replies.

"It didn't used to be this often. I'll have to ask Aaron about boys and beer," her voice trails off.

Jonathan and Henry arrive at a parking lot and park hurriedly.

Henry opens the back door, throws the tattered blanket back, and grabs two bundles. Jonathan takes his pack from Henry as they hurry to the buildings.

"By the way, Moriah made me promise to give you a hug for her," Jonathan says, running.

Henry looks at Jonathan as if to say, 'Really! You can't be serious!' Out loud, he says, "You know I don't do mushy! Just tell her you did!"

"I can't do that. I promised. What good is my word if I don't keep all my promises?" Jonathan stops running.

Henry knew there was no getting around this one, so he reaches over and grabs Jonathan's hand, at the same time he says, "Look here, this is a 'We-are-running-late-and-I-don't-have-time-for-this-shit-MAN-HUG,' okay?!" and he promptly bumps opposite shoulders with Jonathan.

Jonathan says with satisfaction, "Good one, that totally works!"

"Now, come on!" Henry urges, "We can't be late on the last day of class. We need those certificates," as he ducks into a classroom.

Jonathan runs upstairs to another door, pauses briefly to collect himself, then slowly makes his entrance.

PROTECTS

Early the following morning, Jonathan talks to Moriah as they get ready to go to the ranch. While she puts her shoes on, he hauls her new favorite toys through the mudroom towards the car.

"Alright, let's try showing everyone all those things you can do on your own."

"You mean, 'independently?'"

"Yes, that's a big word. I'm impressed."

"It's not that big a word. It's only got five syllables. I know an even bigger one, Mrs. Pingrey taught me."

"Yeah?" Jonathan says with anticipation as he ushers her out to the car.

Meanwhile, Aaron rides to a ranch not far from his own, where he meets with a lawyer-friend to pick up some papers. Aaron confesses, "I didn't think how important it was until that day, last week."

"Glad to be of help," says the lawyer.
"Thanks. How much do I owe you?"

"How about a day of fishing on your river? I'll bring the family."

"But, you are welcome anytime."

"Then, we are more than even, my friend," she assures him.

"I'd better go. I've invited them over to give them the news. I'll have to tell Mrs. Pingrey when she gets back." Aaron bids her goodbye and rides his motorcycle home to greet Marion and the others.

About midday at the ranch, Aaron and Marion with their sleeves rolled high, give their arms a good wash. Although very tired, they are both very pleased. Aaron hands her a towel. "Thank you, Marion, for your help."

"I should thank you for a very exhilarating morning. I quite enjoy that kind of hard work. You might say, I'm drawn to it," she says, wiping her brow.

"I tend to do that."

"What?"

"Attract people who enjoy hard work." He flashes her a grin.

"You mean, you invite them to your ranch for breakfast *and* supper so they can volunteer to help you all day." She nudges him with her shoulder as they both walk away laughing.

From the horse stalls they make their way towards the pigpens where Jonathan and Henry are working, and Moriah is playing with her birthday presents, a small bicycle and her Teddy from

Aaron. Marion warns Moriah to be careful and *not* to stick her fingers in the pig's stall. "Becka is very protective of her piglets, alright?"

"Yes, Nanna."

"Jonathan? Henry? We'll be at the main house."

"Alright," they both look up briefly to reply, then resume working.

Moriah continues playing nearby with her bicycle, pretending to be on horseback and imagining Teddy is an acrobat, jumping into the air, and landing in her basket with great precision. She squeals every time he lands and yells, "Henry!" or sometimes, "Pappy, look!" And every now and then, one or the other would glance over and praise Teddy for a such a fine feat.

Meanwhile, at the kitchen island that doubles as a breakfast bar, Aaron and Marion quench their thirst. Aaron's voice turns serious. "Listen Marion, ahem," he looks at her intently and says, "There's something I have to ask you, or tell you, depending on how you look at it, I suppose. But I don't quite know how to put it."

"You can ask me anything. What can I do for you?" she smiles at him openly.

"It's not what you can do for me," he collects himself, takes a breath and says, "This is something I'd like to do for you. I've thought about it carefully, and I could just let you find out," Her smile never fades because she trusts him implicitly, but now her eyes reflect her compounding bewilderment because the more Aaron explains the more she is puzzled.

"But," and he clasps her hand in both of his, and says very endearingly, "but I'd much rather let you know." He reaches for a drawer nearby but suddenly, the phone rings.

While Aaron and Marion are talking at the main house, Henry and Jonathan continue their work as they keep an eye on Moriah. Moriah miscalculates and Teddy ends up inside the pigpen. Moriah calls out to Henry, but he doesn't answer because he had just put on ear buds to listen to music. From around the bend, where he can't see them, Jonathan hears her call out Henry's name, so he pauses but resumes his work, assuming Henry is taking care of it.

Moriah eyes Teddy on the ground on the other side of the gate, inside the pen. Just then, Moriah remembers earlier that day when Jonathan was telling her that she really should try being a little more independent and not ask Henry to do everything for her like tie her shoes and fetch her things. Moriah decides to be more independent today.

Moments later, inside the pen, as Moriah is about to pick Teddy up from the ground, Becka spots Moriah between her and her piglets. As Becka charges towards her, Moriah stands tall, holds out her hand and declares, "Becka, Stop! Becka, Sit!" the very same way she has seen Mrs. Pingrey command Sadie, her Pekingese. Becka defies Moriah's hand signals and continues charging so Moriah bolts in the opposite direction, not realizing it is in the direction of the piglets! This only makes Becka charge faster.

Moriah yells, "Pappy!"

Jonathan, who is at the other side of the building, hears her, looks up but waits. "Henry!" he hears her call out. Again, he resumes his task because he assumes Henry must be there. What Jonathan hears next comes like electricity through his veins. In her best danger voice, Moriah screams, "Daddyyyy!"

As he runs frantically towards her screams, he hollers, "Henry? Henry? Where's Moriah? HENRY!"

Henry doesn't hear the screaming and continues with the task at hand. He finally notices Jonathan running in his direction, waving his arms like a madman. Instinctively, Henry turns around to look for Moriah, rips off his earphones and only then hears her screams. Without having to think, Henry leaps over the wall and runs to her. But when he picks her up, he realizes there is no time to run no matter the direction he chooses, and furthermore, with the piglets running amok, he could trip and fall, putting Moriah in graver danger. So Henry stands his ground and holds her as high as he could. Becka closes in. Henry tries to control his fear of the impending doom. He holds Moriah tighter, and turns her away from Becka. Just inches away from Henry's legs, Becka stops suddenly and runs the other way. Jonathan had scaled the wall, picked up one of the piglets and is now running frantically from them, leading Becka away.

"Get out! Get Out!" Jonathan hollers, "GET OUT!" He keeps hollering as he runs carrying Becka's scared baby in the opposite direction.

Eventually, on the other side, Henry gets on his knees and hugs Moriah. For all his control in the middle of the pen, now that the danger is gone, Henry feels warm panic flood through him. He holds her close as he catches his breath, and begs his head to stop spinning. Meanwhile, Jonathan arrives from around the bend, out of breath and kneels before Moriah. Only then does Henry let go. Jonathan hugs her and then asks her, "Did Becka hurt you?"

Moriah shakes her head, "No."

But after taking a quick look, Jonathan makes a discovery, and he says very calmly, "Henry, call the doctor."

"What do I say?"

"Tell them to come, and, shshsh." He motions to Henry, then turns his palm toward him. There's blood on Jonathan's fingers. Panic floods Henry's eyes again.

Suddenly at the main house, where Aaron and Marion were talking, Aaron's phone rings, startling Marion, but annoying Aaron. "I'll just silence that," he says as he furrows his brow. Marion stops him, "Aaron, you forget, you're a doctor."
Aaron is taken aback by her admonishing but gentle words and he answers the call. Marion hears urgent yelling from the phone. Her eyes flicker towards the voice as she sips from her cup.
A distraught Henry, at the other end, blurts out, "Doctor, it's Moriah. She got into the pen! We got her out."
"Is she alright?" Aaron says, rising to his feet.

Henry turns away so Moriah won't hear, and under his breath says into the phone, "There's blood!"
"We'll be right there!" Aaron exclaims as he grabs Marion by the arm and they rush out the back door.

"Moriah!" Marion's throat tightens, "What's happened to her, Aaron?" But before Aaron could answer, they see the boys coming towards them in the distance with Moriah cradled in

Jonathan's arms, and Henry holding a rag over her lower leg. Once Marion could see Moriah's eyes, she breathed a sigh of relief.

"I'm sorry. I don't know how she got into the pen. I'm sorry!" Henry repeats as Jonathan surrenders her to Aaron's arms.

Aaron gently sets her down on her feet. "Are you hurt anywhere else, Moriah?" he says and looks her over. She shakes her head, "No," to everyone's relief. Aaron's fears dissipate as he wraps his big burly arms around her. The color returning to his face as he holds her, betray that he is reassuring himself more than he is Moriah, that she is safe and not seriously injured. Off to one side, meanwhile, Jonathan reassures Henry who is besought with guilt. Marion gives Moriah a kiss on the head as she is held captive in Aaron's arms.

"Let's go to the house and bind up that leg." Aaron relinquishes her to Jonathan but motions to him to allow Henry to carry her into the house.

As they walk behind Henry and Moriah, they notice *Moriah whispering* into Henry's ear.

As Moriah sits at the edge of the breakfast bar, Aaron wraps her calf with a bandage. "You've been very brave. We'll have to fix that gate. Do you understand, Moriah, that Becka doesn't normally want to hurt you or anyone, right?"

"Yes, I know. She was just protecting her babies. Like Henry did when he picked me up and held me real tight."

"What's that?" Aaron replies.

Moriah doesn't see, but just then, from where he is sitting, Henry looks towards her. "Henry was protecting me."

As Jonathan and Henry sit in the adjacent room, Aaron takes a deep breath, because now he has to give Moriah a shot. As he prepares it, his hands tremble. Marion notices and he confesses to her with a laugh, "I can't seem to shake it off when I know what I'm about to do will hurt. Distract the boys, will you?"

"Can one of you fetch Teddy?" Marion asks the boys. Henry volunteers. Then she asks, "Jonathan, can you give me a hand?" They make their way to the other room.

Moriah sees Aaron eyeing them as they leave the room. He didn't say a word. He just kept rearranging his accouterments on the table and sighing.

So she touches his arm, to make him bend close. Then she smiles, takes his face in her hands, and *she touches her forehead to his, closes her eyes, and sighs*, "Better?" Soon they both breathe easier.

Aaron chuckles and his hands steady and he gives her the shot. As Jonathan reenters the room he sees Aaron put two fingers to his lips and touch Moriah's now bandaged leg with them making her smile.

Later that evening after supper, Aaron says, "No swimming for a while, Princess. And Marion, let her play if she wants, no need to keep her still."

"Would I do that?" she says as she wraps her arms around Moriah.
"You have," the boys pipe in. "More than once," they add.

She just smiles because she knows they are right.

As the evening wanes, Aaron bids them goodnight, "I'll see you all soon," as he carries a sleepy Moriah out to the car.

Just before they drive off, Marion yells out the window to Aaron, "We'll have to finish our conversation."

He smiles and waves, and when they had turned around the bend he mutters softly, "When the time is right."

Back in his kitchen, as he puts his medical supplies away, Aaron eyes the drawer at the breakfast bar, opens it, and pulls out the documents from the lawyer's office. He eyes the heading,

'Will and Testament of Aaron Phillip Waters.'

While Moriah is sound asleep in the back seat, as they drive back into town, Henry chuckles and says softly, "I should tell you something. She said she climbed on her new bike to reach the latch." Henry chuckles silently.

"Oh," Marion replies, not really surprised.

"and that it wasn't our fault, mine or Jonathan's, and that Jonathan shouldn't get grounded for what happened this time." Still chuckling, Henry blurts out, "And she insisted, neither should I." They all laugh softly.

DANCING AND FISHING

Late that night, after a hard day's work at Aaron's ranch, the boys go to a dance club in the big city. Some friends are already there to meet them when they arrive.

Henry is quite the athletic dancer, showing great strength and agility. The girls around him can't help but ogle even though their boyfriends were obviously jealous.

Jonathan, with a more free-spirited, fun-loving approach to the dance floor is there to have a good time, but seems to be driven by a subtle competitiveness. Jonathan does thrive on feedback though. The more gusto he shows, the more encouragement he gets from the crowd, and he taps into their energy for a wicked cycle that escalates into a wild frenzy and everyone, even Henry, jumps in to join him, enthralled by it all. A little later as they take a break to cool off, the young men strategize.

"Alright then, let them buy the beer if they offer to," pants a confident Henry.
"They always seem too happy to," Jonathan says.
"Yeah, and who's to get in the way of their happiness?"
They both snicker.
And with that, they both plunge into the ocean to go fishing.

After a couple of hours, the boys take a breather from dancing and return to their friends at the table. They don't realize that Aaron is cradling a drink at a table in the back. Momentarily, a girl approaches Jonathan from behind and introduces herself, putting her face close to his ear. He turns towards her. She loses her balance and he catches her around the waist. Again she bends close to say something to him, and he likewise replies. No sooner had he done this, when a giant of a man grabs him by the shoulder and demands he stand up. Out of nowhere, Aaron appears and stands between them. A short brutal exchange ensues, ending with the giant on the floor. Aaron grabs the boys by their collars and drags them with him out into the night air.

"What are you doing here?" the boys ask, surprised.

"I thought you two had each other's backs?" Aaron demands, adrenalin still surging in his veins.

"We do." The boys scratch their heads, and eye their shoes.

"Maybe next time you should watch more carefully. That girl, you do realize she had you pegged?"

"You mean she was interested in....," Jonathan began to say.

"Wrong! Between you and Henry, she picked you out because she knew her boyfriend could take you."

"What!" Jonathan exclaims. "Thanks for the vote of confidence!"

"She made you put your arm around her, right?" Aaron raises his eyebrow. And Jonathan recalls the girl losing balance and his arm reflexively wrapping around her waist. Aaron continues, "Then she says something into your ear so you would do the same."

"Yeah." The boys wonder just how Aaron knew all this.

"All under the watchful eye of her boyfriend," Aaron says amused, but impressed.

"Who, him? How do you know he is her boyfriend?" the boys retort.

Aaron points out to them that as he grabbed them to leave, he saw the girl helping the giant get up from the floor.

"Keep your eyes open before, during, and after a fight. You'll learn a lot." Aaron continues, "It was all very clever, actually, if I hadn't been watching. Boyfriend will be paying more attention to his girl, and they'll be dancing well into the night, just as she planned." Aaron grins at them and starts laughing. Unsure at first, the boys begin laughing, too.

Moments later, as Aaron revs up his bike in the parking lot, Jonathan yells, "Hey, wait a minute, what were you doing here, anyway? How did you know we were here?"

Aaron laughs out loud, and says, "You must think I've nothing better to do than to save your asses so that I don't have to stitch you up!" He rides away, still laughing.

THE PORTAL

Mrs. Pingrey has a favorite spot in her house where she does most of her writing, although she can write just about anywhere and anytime when the urge presents itself. She continues with her line of thought and captures it in ink and traps it on paper before it dissipates like smoke.

"...has unexpectedly torn my heart apart and I bleed old aches that I thought I had put away in a safe place, a place where it wouldn't hurt me anymore, an island called Forgotten. Try as I might, my capsized boat won't right itself. So here I am disoriented and suspended in cold, wet, dark ink. At first, I didn't connect the more recent event with the unspeakable tragedy. 'One had nothing to do with the other,' I told myself. I should have listened to my feelings more than my assurances. It's when I opened my heart to myself that I got a glimpse of the end of a string, snatched it, and pulled it towards me with anticipation and dread. For what lay tethered on the other end of that string, beyond the mysterious unforgiving waters, was yet unknown to me, and I had already acquired the habit of fearing any and all things unknown or lurking in the deep. I implored my hands to stop pulling, to stop reeling what hung on the other end, closer to me. Too close and it could hurt me! But my hands wouldn't listen. I detest being compelled by forces unclear to me. I hate being afraid of the necessary. I do not like cold, wet, dark, when it touches my skin."

"Good morning, Mrs. P. May I come in?" Jonathan's silhouette shows through the glass door.

"Yes, dear, please do."

She continues with the last thought and she scribbles quickly, "Especially when these three are keeping company." The last bit of handwriting, unfortunately, looks rushed. "No matter," she says to herself, "It is important to get it on paper or I might lose it." She fears the pockets of her memory has holes where ideas and thoughts irretrievably slip through too many times without permission.

"Hello, Mrs. P." Jonathan bends down to kiss her on the cheek.

"You are the epitome of etiquette. My house is surely yours, but I do appreciate you calling out ahead or knocking. Who knows, if I were ever having a secret meeting with my clandestine colleagues, and delicate information were to befall your ears, then I may have to tell them to dispose of your body in the river." There is a twinkle in her eye.

"I knew my imagination had to have come from a twistedly creative influence such as yours, Mrs. P."

"You are, indeed, too kind, sir. By the way, I didn't get a chance last night. Welcome home, dear."

"We missed having you. But it's just as well you didn't come. Nothing exciting happened this time." They both laugh.

"What's the matter at hand?"

"Mother needs a tomato."

"What's that again, dear?"

"Mother has requested me to sequester, a bequest of a love apple." Jonathan's face shines with pride.

"Excellent! Quick thinking, too. But you know you needn't come in here to ask for a tomato. I've told your mother many times, you can go in the garden and fetch it and give it to her straight away anytime."

"But, who knows, if I don't come in to ask first, what I might see by accident through the portal to your private abode, Mrs. P." Then he motions to the kitchen window, "Perchance, you and your special prince in a romantic dance?"

She laughs, "In the kitchen, no less! That's a good one, Jonathan. Mind if I borrow it for a future book?"

"Not at all, please do," Jonathan replies while she makes a mental note as they hurriedly make for the garden and the long awaited tomato.

Outside, in the garden, Jonathan asks, "Will you be joining us for dinner and the festival afterwards?"

"Thank you, but, no, not for dinner today, dear. I've already told your Mum. Definitely, we shall meet at the festival though."

"Just so you know Mrs. P., your tomatoes shall once again rescue Mum's salad from a dreadful, even though transient life of drudgery." He throws her a smile then turns towards the house juggling the coveted tomatoes.

Mrs. Pingrey smiles contentedly, 'He's a promising student of words. But, at the very least, he's having fun with it,' she thinks to herself as she watches him walk away.

Once back inside the house, Mrs. Pingrey jots down a few words then closes her notebook. She shall leave her writing for another time. Her train of thought arrested. No regrets, she consoles herself, and delights in the thought that the visit was worth the interruption. Now, to decide what to wear to the festival.

CLOSE YOUR EYES

That afternoon, they all meet at the annual festival in town. As was their tradition, they find a table and enjoy some flavored snowcones. Jonathan wipes Moriah's sticky hands and face, while Mrs. Pingrey holds her half-finished cone. Jonathan has an especially voracious appetite for snowcones and after eating Moriah's leftovers, he asks for everyone else's, first Marion's and Aaron's. Then Mrs. Pingrey offers him hers. He comments between slurps, "You know, I read that somewhere in the Pacific there is a culture that believes that when you eat someone's leftovers, that person can't help but be more endearing to you?" and he tilts his head at Mrs. Pingrey with theatrically soulful eyes as he scarfs down the rest of her snowcone. She smiles at him.

Marion quips, "Is that why you ate Aaron's leftovers?" Aaron chuckles.

Jonathan chokes a little, "Nawww! I meant Moriah's, and yours, and..."

Just then, Henry rushes up to him, hands him his snowcone, and takes a debonair-ish pose with his hand resting on the table. "Here, take this, come on!" he quickly says to Jonathan who reflexively accepts it but protests.

“Now, you're making fun of me!” Jonathan says, miffed.

“What? What are you talking about? I just want you to hold it for a second.” Henry never removes his gaze from the two young ladies who are walking by in the distance but are looking towards him.

Henry tries his suave grin on them and in the meantime, talks through his teeth to Jonathan, “Snowcones just don't look cool unless she's got one too.”

Jonathan sees the girls smile at Henry. Then it dawns on him that now, he looks doubly uncool with a snowcone in each hand.

Forever the imp in Henry's life, Jonathan inverts the snowcone onto the back of Henry's hand. Henry jumps from the cold mess. And the girls in the distance react with pity mixed with amusement and walk away giggling at Henry's expense.

After a little while, the boys ask to borrow Moriah for a bit.

“We have a surprise for her. You know, like we do every year.”

“To honor her birthday, even though it was two days ago.” They grin at each other.

“You have to close your eyes, Moriah,” Jonathan says to Moriah as he carries her to the large fountain nearby. When she covers her eyes, Henry reveals to the others the gossamer fairy wings he was hiding behind his back. They both help her put on her wings and kneel before her, each taking one hand.

Marion, Aaron, and Mrs. Pingrey watch from a distance, and recall the past years when they had witnessed this special event on the bridge near the waterfall.

Later that night, Aaron carries a tired, sleeping Moriah upstairs to her bed. Marion removes her crumpled wings and her shoes before they tuck her in.

“No jammies?” Aaron asks.

“More important to sleep in her festival dress than to stay awake in her jammies. School day tomorrow,” Marion says softly as they tiptoe out of Moriah's room to join the others downstairs.

HEADING HOME

The following day, the engine of the car cuts as Jonathan approaches the schoolyard. The car rolls to a stop. This time only Jonathan creeps up behind Moriah, covers her eyes, and whispers, “Guess who?”

She gasps suddenly then exclaims, “Pappy!” as she turns to hug him. “Where’s Henry?”

“He’s…” At a loss for words, Jonathan ponders his choice delicately. After a moment, he blurts out, “Indisposed!” and smiles, pleased.

“You mean, he’s asking a girl out,” she announces perceptively and they both grin. “Can I sit in Henry’s spot?” she asks as she skips towards the car.

“Yes.”

Moriah sits up front next to Jonathan, and adjusts the seat and seatbelt herself. Then Jonathan throws her stuff in the back seat. They land next to Teddy who, wisely, has his seatbelt fastened.
“Hey, hang on! What do you know about boys and girls?” his tone, suspicious.

“Oh, stuff.”

He rolls his eyes and shakes his head. He's going to have to ask his mother about how to handle this. Instead of heading home to drop her off first, Jonathan proposes a slight detour.

"Look here, he's probably done. Let's go pick him up, alright?"

In a little while, they pull up alongside a very happy Henry and he hops in the back.

"Henry," says Moriah, "do you want your seat?"

"No, I'll sit in your seat, so I can do *this*," he says as he puts his hands over her eyes.
Then he hisses deviously into her ear, "Guess who?"

Moriah puts her hands over his. Pretending to be stumped, she waits a moment. Then suddenly she shrieks, "Pappy!" to their great amusement.

"Clever girl!" Henry says, tickling her neck and making her shriek again. They laugh uproariously as Jonathan puts the car into gear, and pulls away from the curb. As they continue laughing...

CHAPTER 2 CAPSIZED and SUSPENDED

OPEN YOUR EYES

The door next to where Moriah sits is violently smashed without warning by a large farm truck carrying flammable fuel. Moriah's head strikes the window. There is another crash, farther, dimmer, and yet another. Their car finally stops skidding sideways but then the truck bursts into flames. Moriah and Jonathan are unconscious. Henry is dazed but comes to his senses, and tries to open his door.

"Moriah! Jonathan! Moriah!" he screams.

After several attempts at kicking his door open, he escapes through the door behind Jonathan's, knocking Teddy out onto the ground. He runs to the other side and frantically tries to open Moriah's door, but it is crumpled and stuck. Then he comes around and tries to rouse Jonathan to no avail.
"Jonathan! Jonathan! You've got to help me get her out!" There is an explosion very close to Moriah. So Henry again tries to get her out by prying the door open. As strong as his is, he isn't strong enough to open it.

Then he realizes there is another way. He breaks the window with shrapnel from the truck and he reaches into the cab to release the lever that reclines the back of Moriah's seat. Then he enters through the other door and frees her from the crumpled metal and is able to lift her limp body out and away from danger.

With her eyes closed and with one hand over Henry's hand, she whispers in his ear,

"Henry," just before he lays her on the side of the road.

He runs back just in time to drag Jonathan out before flames engulf the car. Jonathan rouses and Henry helps him to Moriah's side. Henry lays Moriah in Jonathan's arms before running off to rescue others injured in the accident.

Jonathan sits on the pavement and cradles Moriah from behind, calling out her name over and over increasingly louder between sobs. He has one hand over the side of her head where it struck the glass. The other he has around her chest. Then he realizes that between sobs, he can hear her breathing, so Jonathan stops calling out her name, and swallows his sobs.

Now Jonathan doesn't hear anything around him, only Moriah's breathing, fast and shallow. His chest heaves as his fears begin to surface in swells. He tries to stifle it. Moriah's eyes remain closed. When Jonathan moves his hand across to her forehead, Moriah, with eyes closed, reaches up with a weak hand and pulls his hand over her closed eyes. Jonathan knew what she was doing but could not fathom why.

He could only hear her breathing, slower now, not so shallow, but more deliberate and with purpose. He bends down to bring his face close to her ear and whispers. Time slows to a crawl as his trembling lips usher the words into the chaos. The din swallows the sound, but his lips say it all.

"Guess who."

Moriah takes a breath, the deepest she could muster. Her mouth caressing the word, she whispers to Jonathan,

"Pappy," as her last breath parted from her little lips.

Jonathan screams, "Henry! HENRY!" In the distance, as Henry gently helps an elderly man sit on the ground at the edge of the road, he says, "Help is on the way." Then he rushes to Jonathan and Moriah. Realizing she is not breathing, he tries to revive her. Jonathan stays close and watches Henry try again and again.

Shaking his head, Henry sits back on his heels and gasps, "No!" Then Henry holds Moriah's face in his hands. "Moriah, please, open your eyes." She remains motionless. Then Henry sucks in a quivering breath as his tears fall on Moriah's wrist. Feeling a tug on his sleeve, Henry helps Moriah back into Jonathan's arms and puts her hands over Jonathan's. He pulls his hands back and lays them on his lap, palms up, but stays very near, just within reach.

The sounds of reality relentlessly beat their fists on the door of Jonathan's consciousness. There is chaos all around but all Jonathan hears now is the stillness that lay in his arms, the darkness that has buried his sobs, the silence of the abyss that has swallowed him whole.

Jonathan's face is stone. But as the firemen, and paramedics approach, his face becomes contorted and he stretches his hand out,

"Stay away! Don't come near. You can't help us! Stay away!" He screams. Then he begs, "Please, don't take her!"

Henry who is closer to the firemen and paramedics, stands, shakes his head and says two words that make them stop where they stood. Finding his voice, he makes it penetrate the veil of tears, and says, "I tried."

The paramedics step back. They know they don't have to check Moriah's pulse. Henry falls to his knees onto the pavement and puts his hands to his bowed head, shoulders shaking. One of the paramedics puts his hand on Henry's shoulder. Others nearby take their helmets off. Some look at Henry, some look away.

No one could bring themselves to look at Moriah.

Eventually, the paramedics come back for Moriah and ask to take her away. Jonathan wouldn't let go. Henry asks them if they could wait a while. After a while, Henry talks Jonathan into letting her go but instead of putting her on the gurney, Jonathan gives her to Henry, who drops to his knee. He realizes now, he couldn't bear to let her go. Jonathan kneels beside Henry and Moriah.

"Why?" Henry says through his tears. Jonathan replies with silence.

Eventually, Jonathan stands up and helps Henry stand, and they both carry Moriah onto a gurney so the paramedics can take her away. When the paramedics try to cover her face with the blanket, Jonathan whispers, "No! Please, don't. Please," he implores them to spare them the pain.

So they pull the blanket to reach just under her elbows and tuck it in.

Just as they are about to wheel her away, one of the firemen comes running up with something in his hands. When he is near he motions to Jonathan and Henry, "May I?" and he gently tucks Teddy under Moriah's arm. But before they take her away, another man in uniform, rushes to her side.

As a helicopter in the background rises into the air, Jonathan sits at the open end of an ambulance. His face an empty vessel. Henry is nearby sobbing. Henry's gaze falls on Jonathan. He sees him through his tears. Jonathan on the other hand, sees no one and hears nothing.

ECHOES

Aaron hurries to the hospital on his motorcycle. After a couple of close calls, he takes his third spill right in front of a police car. The sympathetic officer escorts Aaron to the emergency doors, then bows his head as Aaron dashes away.

From the end of the hall outside the room where they are keeping Moriah, Aaron sees a familiar figure through the glass wall. The man in uniform, facing the curtain around the bed, was talking into his phone. “Yes, I want to be here to meet him when he arrives....No, I don't know what to say....I will. Hug the kids for me. ....Yes, I'll be home soon.”

“I'll be here, Gregory,” she replies.

He hangs up and wipes his face with his wrist. Then he turns around just as Aaron rushes in through the doorway. Aaron stops abruptly and turns to the glass wall, laying his hands on it in a feeble attempt to hold himself up. He can't bring himself to turn around to face his friend. Behind his friend hung the curtain, and beyond the curtain a nightmare he was certain he couldn't endure. Gregory approaches him silently, sits near him on the cold floor, and puts a warm arm around his shuddering shoulder.

Alone now, Aaron pushes his heavy body past a metal fire door into the stairwell, still clinging to Teddy with one arm, his back to the wall. A chill fills the walls of the hospital's spine as the stairwell reverberates with echoes of Aaron's sobs as he staggers to the foot of the stairs.

Later that evening, with bowed shoulders, Gregory comes home to his wife. He tells her, "I got the call, but didn't know until I saw them." Then he saw Teddy, so he ran to the gurney just before the paramedics were about to lift Moriah onto the ambulance. Trembling, he said to them, "Please, please. She's family. She's my daughter's best friend." They help Gregory put her gently into his helicopter.

That day, Moriah left Henry and Jonathan on wings, with Gregory to watch over her and escort her away, safely to the sky, where she was welcomed with open arms by kind faces in white garment.

NOT THERE

A helicopter flies overhead and a little girl's hand reaches out the window to release flower petals. The petals drift from above, down to the people gathered below. They move slowly, in flows, like water around rocks, around where Moriah lay, around Jonathan. As he sat there for a long time, the people continued to flow around him, until they were gone. And again at the reception, he sat there, the same, like a stone jutting just above the surface, water flowing around it, people flowing around him. Touching him as they pass, but not knowing how to touch him. Time passes him by, unchanged, not feeling, not knowing, not sensing the flow around him. There is a lot of handshaking, hugging, some wiping of tears, and scattered phrases, "Sorry for your loss."...."If there's anything we can do." Henry is attentive to Marion and politely engaged with the guests, while Jonathan's face is a blank stare looking past and through what's before him even as he shakes their hands, even as he reaches out to touch the water that flowed past. The water runs through his hand, through the ghost of one who is not there.

At Marion's house, that evening there's more hand shaking, hugging and people leaving with luggage. The cacophony of funeral and reception sounds whirling around in the air that day cascade down and find a home in Jonathan's head, an avalanche, a deafening roar. He retreats upstairs to escape it to no avail. It was only when exhaustion overcame his body that his eyes and ears found respite, only for his soul to be thrust again into reality when he awoke to his curse the next day.

The house is eerily quiet. Marion comes around the stairs, and walks past the dining room with an armful of beddings from the guest room. She loads the wash. Then later puts dishes away in the kitchen, and turns the heat on for the kettle. Soon it is whistling, competing with the washer's hum for attention. As she pours water for tea she jumps when the phone rings. She picks up a call for Jonathan. It's his boss, Paula.

"I am truly sorry, Paula. Someone here should have called you."

"It's alright, Marion, I understand. He can come when he's ready. It won't be the same with him not here, but right now he needs to be there."

"Thank you," Marion says, relieved. They hang up. Then, Marion talks to Jonathan and persuades him to have some breakfast. He obeys as if he had no mind of his own.

Aaron calls to check up on Jonathan, but also asks, "By the way, Mrs. Pingrey, how's Henry? We'll have to keep an eye on him, too."

Mrs. Pingrey tells Aaron, "Henry says he'll be better off going to work than not." That day Henry stops by after hours, still in his paramedic uniform, and offers to help Marion with Jonathan's chores. "Or anything," he says, with his head low, "to lighten the load. I'll come after work." And so he does. And when he's done helping, he always stays a while to sit on the floor in Jonathan's room, even though Jonathan doesn't talk to him.

Aaron, too, visits. He says he's looking in on Jonathan, but talks to Marion and Mrs. Pingrey until very late, and leaves only when he gets called away to the hospital. Sometimes he makes tea for them. Clumsily at first, not being accustomed to the dainty little porcelain cups. Once, he overflowed his and was left with not enough for the last one. So, he did what any fair and just friend would do, and using his cup, evened the portions out among all the cups so in the end, no one would be left lacking.

For Aaron's benefit, Marion doesn't let on that Moriah's passing has caused a deep rift where old aches have surfaced and now stir her heart. Once, though, Marion does find occasion to share some thoughts with Mrs. Pingrey.

Marion and Mrs. Pingrey revisit a time when Marion is much younger. There is a clown with a bouquet of balloons but they are frozen in time and space in Marion's mind. There are sounds of musical toys playing in the background, and there is a little girl's voice, laughing, playing. Marion knows that going to this place will make her lose tears, but one thing she also knows she can rely on, it's that Mrs. Pingrey's shoulder can bear both their tears.

Every now and then, but only when she really has to, Mrs. Pingrey calls a dear friend just to feel his voice embrace her sad heart even though he is half a world away. Just knowing he was sad with her was enough.

AFRAID TO STEP AWAY

Over the next few days, though, Jonathan eventually is slow to respond when talked to. He spends more and more time alone with his thoughts, some days not leaving his room or getting up from his chair. Marion and Mrs. Pingrey do their best. But as Jonathan sinks, Marion becomes more vigilant. So much so, she refuses to leave the room and a worried Mrs. Pingrey talks to Aaron. “Henry and I are worried about her, Aaron.”

“Have Henry call me, please. I’m on my way, but just the same, please have him call me.”

As Mrs. Pingrey suggests, Henry calls Aaron. “Doctor, she refuses to leave his side. It's as if she's afraid something bad will happen if she steps away. I can't get through to her. Mrs. Pingrey has tried everything.”

Aaron talking into the telephone receiver in his bike helmet, says, “I'll be there in a few minutes. Listen, Henry, have you got your leathers and gear there or at your own place? I'll need them.”

Soon after, Henry greets Aaron as he climbs up the stairs. “Maybe if you just talk to her.”

“I've got a better idea.” Aaron says with a confident smile. Henry grabs Aaron's arm just before he enters Jonathan's room. “I can't thank you enough.”

“What, this? I should be thanking you for letting me do this,” Aaron replies, then ducks into the room, and gently takes hold of Marion's elbow, and urges her to come with him. Henry hands the gear to Aaron, who promptly gives it to Marion. “Try these on. You're coming with me,” he tells her.

“But,” she protests.

“Doctor's orders, end of discussion,” he says firmly in a whisper.

Henry could hear, and relaxes knowing, 'Aaron's got this.'

Marion glances at Henry imploring him for moral support and instead,

Henry says, “You're in good hands. I couldn't vouch for anyone better.”

Henry gives her a reassuring kiss, and continues in a parental tone, “Now you two, be careful.” Then he puts a hand to Aaron's arm, and in a low voice says, “I'm trusting you on this.”

TO SPEAK OF HER AGAIN

They mount Aaron's motorcycle. “Come on. You know you need this,” Aaron says into the microphone in his helmet.

Marion nods, and replies, “Alright, you win.”

Before long, they reach the end of town, and small farms whisk by. Marion starts to weep, softly, at first. Aaron can hear her through the microphone and feel her sobbing. He puts his hand over hers and says, “Do you want me to stop or turn back? I'll not do this if it upsets you.”

“No, it's fine. Let's continue ahead. Just take me far away.”

“Alright.” He pats her hand reassuringly. “Just a little farther.”
Aaron stops near a river, by a tree, and helps her with her helmet.
“We'll get through this, Marion. We'll keep an eye on him.
I won't let anything happen to him, I promise.”

Marion cries louder.

“What did I say? What's wrong?” He waits until it subsides. Then he holds her shoulders at arm's length. “Talk to me,” insisting, he adds, “Marion, you know you can tell me anything.”

“Thallia,” she said through her tears.

Aaron's world spins. Reawakened horror and anguish intertwine in his heart.

They both remember that day long ago. A young Marion screams at a young Aaron and shoves him away with both hands, "Don't you ever say that name aloud before me again! Leave me! Just leave!" And a morose Aaron leaves abruptly.

Back by the river, Aaron puts his hand on the motorcycle to steady himself. Marion puts her arm over his slumped shoulders. They remain silent for a while. Finally, they talk. The wind blows through the sky urging the clouds to move on by as they sit on the grass on a rise, facing the river, the sun caressing the hills, silently bidding them goodnight.

Marion says, "I never meant to hurt you, and I never meant for what happened to come between us."

"I thought you'd never allow me to speak of her again," he says softly, his grateful tears washing away the heaviness on his heart.

GREAT NEED

On the way home, Marion and Aaron have lighter faces. Marion breaks the silence, "Dare I ask?" she says as she recalls the name so prominently painted on the motorcycle's gas tank.

"Don't ever hesitate to ask me anything."

"Who in the world is Alexandria?" she asks slowly, unsure of his reaction.

He grins as if he had wanted to hear this long ago. "Are you jealous?"

"No, is there reason to be?" She winced at her choice of words. They reveal too much.

"She was very close to my heart. The time I was away, in South America. You remember?"

"Yes, I remember South America." Her eyes grow sad.

"You know I've wanted to tell you. You wouldn't let me, remember? I tried a whole year ago?"

Marion had tried to forget, but the memory of that day lingers. The wind was blowing. "Let me tell you about her," Aaron implores her, his hand resting on the gas tank next to the name.

"I don't want to know. And you don't owe me an explanation. Let's just leave it at that," Marion says, holding her hair away from her face, and wishing he would never bring it up again.

Interrupting her thoughts, Aaron continues, "We got along very well. You would have liked her."

"Hmm, I know your taste," Marion chooses a polite but neutral response.

"She only ever showed me unconditional love, and was very loyal."

"You mean faithful," corrected Marion, but Aaron doesn't seem to hear her and continues reminiscing,

"She was all I had, at a time of great need." His face grew somber as he remembers the day he left her.

"Do I really need to know all this?" Marion starts to fidget.

"You're doing it again Marion, closing the door on me."

"Alright, I'll listen." But her eyes veer away, 'She couldn't escape his confession, but she didn't have to like it,' she decided.

"She saved me. I wish I hadn't left her."

"Why did you?"

"I had to leave her with someone who needed her more," his voice grows sadder still.

Aaron is reminded of the bittersweet memories from that rainy day long ago. Aaron is leaving on a canoe, waving goodbye to a woman on shore. Next to her, a man with his hands on a boy's shoulder. They are standing on a dock, with a dog dashing to and fro on the muddy river banks in South America. This day particularly, Aaron is grateful for the warm rain, a jungle camouflage.

It is dark now as they approach the front of the house. Aaron and Marion dismount the motorcycle, and Aaron greets Mrs. Pingrey who is checking the mailbox. Marion slams the helmet into Aaron's belly and exclaims under her breath, "You idiot!"

"Oof!" Aaron is caught off guard but then begins to chuckle.
Marion marches towards the house.
Mrs. Pingrey throws a bewildered glance at Aaron, "Explain?"

Aaron says to Mrs. Pingrey, "We had a long talk. It was good, very good. But on the way home, she happened to ask. She knows about Alexandria now."
"You mean all this time, she never…"
"Nope. She wouldn't let me tell her."

Mrs. Pingrey and Aaron laugh softly and look towards Marion with kind eyes. Marion who had taken a few strides towards the house, turns around, sees them laughing and starts to laugh lightly, then under her breath she repeats, "You idiot!"
Meanwhile, Aaron tucks his keys away, but hanging out of his pocket dangles a sterling keychain in the shape of a shiny Labrador.

GINGERLY

In the days that followed, Marion and Mrs. Pingrey tend to Jonathan as gingerly as they can. Jonathan stays in his room and doesn't talk to anyone for a long while. He just stares out in front of him at nothing in particular. Aaron offers Marion a number to a colleague.

"If you think it would help, give him a call. I'm probably not the best one to help Jonathan in this capacity. And by the way, Marion, if you have Henry come help to watch him, we can keep an eye on both of them."

Mrs. Pingrey, every now and then offers Jonathan something to eat. "Just open your mouth, Jonathan. It's your favorite," says Mrs. Pingrey.
Jonathan turns the other way.

Later, Marion pushes Jonathan gently through the bathroom door. He seems frozen. When she returns after several minutes, he is standing where she had left him except he had turned to face the wall where he had leaned forward until his forehead touched it. The cold surface touching his skin seems a distant reminder of this world's reality. Marion decides to ask for Henry's help. “I think if you can just get him to stand in the shower and turn the water on, he’ll do the rest,” she said, unsure.

Henry does his best. After a long wait, and several occasions of alarming falling sounds through the door, a silent Jonathan emerges from the bathroom smelling much cleaner. It doesn’t seem to matter much to Jonathan, but it seems to make Marion a lot happier. As Marion ushers him back to his room, she sees an exhausted Henry, drenched through and through, standing at the bathroom doorway, wincing and rubbing the back of his head.

YOU ARE NOT ALONE

After a while, Marion calls Aaron on the phone. She is at a loss. She tells him she hesitates to call the other doctor whom Jonathan doesn't even know.

"Mrs. Pingrey says, 'Jonathan will let us know what he needs when he's ready.' Surely, it has been too long? I don't know if I'm doing things right."

Aaron tries to allay her fears, "Take heart, Marion. I'll be there as soon as I can."

Soon after the call, Aaron comes to the house to visit Jonathan. Henry surrenders his chair to Aaron, and leaves to go downstairs. Just outside the room, Marion whispers to Henry, "I'll make tea. Can you bring some up for Aaron?"

Aaron, in the meantime, tells Jonathan a story that he has never told anyone before. Aaron speaks openly, "I know a man who met with a terrible tragedy, such a one that you would not expect anyone to endure. This man was plunged into the cold dark waters. He thought, the end must be near, for I am alone. He did not reach his hand outward because he did not believe anyone would reach out to take it. He felt himself drifting deeper into the cold. But, before long, a hand reached out to him and grabbed him by the hair, and pulled him up, and that same hand brought him back from the depths, and pushed life back into his chest so that he could live another day."

Henry returns with the tea and pauses just outside Jonathan's doorway.

Aaron continues, "The next day he decided, the next time he thinks he is drowning and alone, not to believe what his senses tell him but instead to cling to what his heart urges him to believe. Jonathan," Aaron leans closer, "This is your family pulling you by the hair. Help us. Do not push our hand away. Once you've come up for air, then you can decide what your heart tells you. You can decide whether or not you are alone."

When Aaron spoke no more, Henry entered and offered him his cup. "Thank you," they say to each other at the same time. Then Henry leaves Aaron with Jonathan. As he sips from his cup, Aaron decides it's not necessary to tell Jonathan or Henry about the shimmering mermaid giving the man she rescued a kiss before she went away.

That evening there is an inconsolable sadness in Marion's eyes as she prepares to leave Jonathan. She puts her lips to his head and whispers, "Remember, I love you." But before she leaves, Mrs. Pingrey holds Marion's hand in both of hers. "You are this family's provider, Marion. This, too, is important."

"Oh, Wynefred, I couldn't do this without you."

"And you won't have to," she gives a reassuring smile that quells Marion's fears just long enough for Marion to get herself out to the car.

Mrs. Pingrey watches the car pull away, then turns from the window back to her charge. The smile she so confidently displayed for Marion has left her. She remembers that Jonathan's bowl remains untouched. In all the years of caring for him, this little concoction had always been her secret weapon in her arsenal against all that had ever ailed him in body or in spirit as a child. She recalls that in the past, watching him eat it was strangely reassuring that she was winning the battle. Seeing the full bowl today was a harsh reminder that she was failing him. Not knowing what else to try, she settles into a chair next to his bed, and takes his hand and squeezes it.

The clock's tired face drooped sleepily. Henry brings supper up for himself and for Mrs. Pingrey, and she urges him to eat without her. "I'll have mine later," she says.
But Henry refuses to take a bite until Mrs. Pingrey agrees to join him. "I'll eat if you do," he bargains with her.

She says, "Can you help me turn him, then we can both have supper, and then figure out who should sit with him next? If we both stay up, we'll both be tired. If we time things right, we may get by without bringing Lance in to help this time."

"Sounds good." Henry helps her turn him. Jonathan stirs a little then lies motionless facing away from them.

SAFE HARBOR

As they settle in for a bedside meal, Mrs. Pingrey changes gear, and her eyes fall on her other charge. "Tell me Henry, anything interesting happen at work today? You know how I love your adventures." Jonathan, having the advantage of facing the other way, has his eyes open as Henry and Mrs. Pingrey talk.

Henry tells her about a rescue. Although the rescue ended well, Henry looks troubled.

"Would you like to share with me what is troubling you, Henry?" she says very gingerly.

"Not tonight, Mrs. P." He looks towards the door and rises quietly. "Maybe another time?"

"Just say the word, Henry," she offers tenderly.

Henry reaches over and gives her a sideways hug, then offers to take their trays downstairs.

Mrs. Pingrey hands him hers. "He's asleep. I can take the first turn if you care to lie down. You must be tired from work. But I'd like to try giving him something to eat. This used to work for everything." She hands him the full bowl. "Any suggestions?"

“I’ve got an idea,” he says with a twinkle in his eye. “I don’t know if I can make it the way he does, but I’ll bring up ‘The Cannonball!’”

A very proud Henry brings up a bowl, but leaves to go to sleep downstairs. Mrs. Pingrey sits on the bed and shakes Jonathan’s shoulder. She whispers a few words into his ear. Time slows as her lips mouth a few words, and Jonathan blinks and turns towards her.

“Here, Jonathan, sit up for me. Henry made you your newest favorite,” Mrs. Pingrey is pleasantly surprised when Jonathan sits up. She tempts him with a spoonful of ‘The Cannonball,' “Just a little, for starters?”

This time he obeys and takes a mouthful. When he had swallowed, she tries to give him another spoonful and he suddenly but gently grabs her wrist. She gasps. Jonathan slowly takes the spoon from her hand and takes another spoonful on his own.

“He’s awake!” exclaims Mrs. Pingrey silently as her heart skips.

His eyes look upwards to meet her gaze. But no sooner has he swallowed, when he starts to want to cry, but he holds back his tears.

“It’s alright, Jonathan. It’s alright.” She wraps her arms around him, as if to say, “Here, dear, a safe harbor for you to stay while you weep. Stay all you want. Weep all you need until the storm leaves your heart.” So that’s what he does for a while. Eats a little and cries, then sleeps a little and cries some more. Sometimes crying himself to sleep.

Mrs. Pingrey calls Aaron to send him word but at the same time just to hear some reassurance. What Aaron tells her, she already knows, but hearing it from him somehow makes her feel better. "Aaron, I know I should be glad, but it's a little scary, all this crying."

"This is actually good news, Wynefred. You said you think he woke up on his own? I think Jonathan has opened up a window for us. Now, we wait for him to open a door. And Wynefred, How's Henry doing?"

"I didn't wake him. He was so tired. He'll be elated, I'm sure. But, Aaron, something is not quite right. We still need to keep an eye on Henry."

Aaron suggests, "With Marion away, this gives you reason to ask him to stay at the house more often when he's not at work. Have you found out yet where he disappears to late at night?" Aaron's brows furrow.

"He's not opening up. I can't try too hard. You know Henry. We might have to use other methods," she said biting a lip.

Mrs. Pingrey doesn't realize that Henry is just outside in the hallway, within earshot of her conversation with Aaron. Henry hears enough, and slowly turns back to the guest room.

Mrs. Pingrey also calls Marion to tell her the news.

"Whatever it is you did or said, thank you, Wynefred," Marion says with much relief.

"I don't know that it was my doing. Henry was with him too. Aaron saw him, and you talked to him before you left. Who knows?"

Just the same, Marion's heart is much lighter for the rest of her trip.

Marion returns from her trip and they resume taking turns sitting up with Jonathan. Now that he is awake, they find the need to be more vigilant. Henry tries to console Jonathan when he starts to cry but each time he does, Henry's eyes well up, too. Stifling it becomes increasingly difficult. So he calls for help and leaves the room. Eventually, leaving the room isn't enough.

NEEDS YOU MORE

Henry runs from the house, into the night rubbing his brow, and breathing hard. Marion grabs the keys from Henry's hands and sits at the wheel. Henry is about to resist, but Marion interjects, "I'll not let you drive upset. If you want, I won't talk," she offers as a compromise.

He surrenders and climbs in the truck. "Please, just go anywhere. I don't care. I just need some air," Henry says as he catches his breath and quells his emotions with great difficulty.

Then after a couple of miles, Marion pulls over and says very gently, "You know it's okay to ask for my help."

"It's alright." His eyes dart sideways. "He needs you."

"And you don't?" Marion replies.

Henry clears his throat, "He needs you more right now." Then he adds, "Please, just let me do this."

Marion gives in and nods.

"Come on," he says with a forced smile, "we're needed at the house."

Marion pulls him closer, "Oh, Enzo, honey," and kisses his temple, "you're so good to him." When they arrive at the front of the house, Marion says with a gleam in her eye, "I have an idea. Maybe it will help."

They decide that from that night onward, Henry stays to watch Jonathan while he sleeps. But, this particular night, Jonathan wakes while Henry is snoring softly on the chair. Jonathan pulls his heavy body from his bed, and stands on unsteady legs, reaches his arm out, and pulls the blanket that had fallen but was clinging to the armrest, to cover Henry, then he crawls back to bed. That night, Jonathan remembers that he had made Henry want to cry. After watching over Henry for a while, Jonathan eventually falls asleep.

HALFWAY UP

Finally, one morning, as Mrs. Pingrey draws the curtains and opens the window. She hears a croak.

“Mrs. P.,” he says in a hoarse voice.

‘The sweet sounds of his first words!’ She savors the moment, and turns to him. “I’m here. I hear you, dear.”

“I’ve lost her. I’ve lost her forever,” he barely whispers. Over the next few days, he slowly opens up and shares his thoughts with Mrs. Pingrey.

“I dream of her, then when I wake up she’s really gone. I don’t want to wake up. I just want to be where she is forever.”

Mrs. Pingrey says some comforting words but Jonathan doesn’t hear it. It is as if his mind is allowing through the gates of his senses, only that which he could assimilate, without too much pain.

“I just want her to come back, I want her to be here. I want things to be the way they were before.”
Mrs. Pingrey tries to be helpful and offers some kind thoughts, but Jonathan only hears a murmur from her lips.

"Sometimes I hear her laughter, or her voice calling out to me, as if she's really here."

Mrs. Pingrey thinks a moment then offers, "Perhaps it is an echo of what once was, an echo of her essence. Jonathan, some echoes are strong."

Jonathan looks up and finally sees and hears Mrs. Pingrey.

The following morning, Jonathan decides to get dressed and come downstairs. Jonathan looks all over for Mrs. Pingrey. Then he thought he'd check upstairs again. As he climbs halfway up the staircase, he spots her, "Mrs. Pingrey, where's Henry? He needs your help!"

"At work, dear." Alarmed, she asks, "How do you know, Jonathan?"

"I don't know how I know, Mrs. P. I just know, Henry needs your help."

"Perhaps, it's not me he needs. Could it be you?"

WORSE

Over breakfast Jonathan says to Marion, "It just feels like there's something he needs to tell me. I don't know. It's just a feeling."

Later that morning, Marion talks to Henry on the phone, something about chopping a fallen tree at the edge of Aaron's ranch.

"You guys can just hang out."

Henry pleads with her, "But I don't know what to say, or do."

"It's alright." Marion tries to ease his anxieties. "Just chop wood," she says, smiling.

On the drive up, Jonathan and Henry, both unsure of what to say, find safety in silence. When they arrive, they decide that Jonathan would start chopping while Henry fetches the wheelbarrow. Jonathan starts slowly at first, methodically. Then with newfound energy, he picks up the pace. He swings the axe again and again forcefully, then aggressively, then violently. He strikes with all his might until he was too weak to lift the axe. It is a terrible sight to behold if not for the tears on his face. Henry thought, from an obscure vantage point behind a tree, if he had not known Jonathan better, the look on his face would have terrified him.

On the way back, in the truck, Henry asks.
"Are you alright?"
"Yeah."
"You're real quiet."
"I'm tired."
"Yeah, that was a lot of wood."
"Tired of thinking."
Henry takes a deep breath. 'Here goes,' he says to himself.
"Want to talk about it?"

Jonathan turns away from Henry, curls up and closes his eyes. "It doesn't matter. None of it matters," he mutters, his eyes still closed, "I couldn't keep her from dying."

Henry murmurs to himself, *"No. It was supposed to be me,"* his eyes haunted by his recurring nightmare. He remembers too much.

But Jonathan doesn't hear Henry's whisper. He doesn't see the change in Henry's face. They go home not talking about anything anymore. When they arrive, Marion senses something is wrong. Jonathan says he feels ill and goes upstairs. But Henry looks much worse off. She asks him to stay for supper so they could talk. Henry is quiet and eats little. She waits. Then after a little while he tells Marion, "I'm sorry, I think I made him worse."

MORE THAN I DESERVE

Jonathan is just about to leave for work when there is a knock on the door. Jonathan answers. It's a stranger.

"Hello," says the elderly man. He wrings his hat in his hands and shifts his weight.

Marion approaches the door. "What can we do for you?"

"Madam, may I introduce myself?" The words seem memorized, but then a burst of emotion explodes from his throat. His demeanor crumbles and he falters, losing his words.
I've come to...I'm sorry. I'm the driver of the," He blurts out the last word, "truck."

Jonathan's face turns morose. The small ember that had been slowly returning to his eyes is snuffed out instantly. His arms drop to his sides and he turns to walk away. Marion puts a hand on his arm. He doesn't turn to face her but he stops.
"I'm sorry, Mother. I've nothing to offer."

He climbs upstairs in a fog. He doesn't realize in his daze he slams into Henry's shoulder at the stairway. Henry is startled. But, Jonathan remains silent and continues on as if nothing happened.

Henry doesn't know what to think. Puzzled and hurt, Henry steals away through the back door, but not before Mrs. Pingrey notices his demeanor. She remembers her conversation with Jonathan about Henry just the other day.

Immediately after Jonathan turns away, the farmer turns to retreat to his car. He stifles sobs. Marion quickly steps out of the doorway and catches his arm. "Please, don't go just yet. Forgive my son. He is not himself. You and I shall sit and talk a while?"

The man faces her and obeys. It seems easier than deciding what to do.

Marion makes tea for herself and the farmer. His shoulders slump over his cup. Marion puts her hand on them as they shake. Later Marion ushers him toward the front door. And the man looks forlornly towards where he last saw Jonathan disappear. He hands her a slip of paper.

"I can't promise much. Just that, it may take time," she says to him.

"You have given me more than I deserve, madam," he nods, tips an imaginary hat, and bids her, "Good day."

That day, more than any other, Jonathan has to force himself not to crawl back into the sanctuary that was his room, and he makes himself go back out into the world. It takes much effort and energy to go to work, but once there, he takes comfort in the familiar faces.

STURDY ONCE AGAIN

After work, Henry enters through Mrs. Pingrey's front door still in his uniform, and he gives her a hug.

“Thanks for doing this for me, Henry.”

Earlier on the phone, she asked Henry to strengthen the supporting braces of her top shelf, even though she is quite proficient with hand tools and owns a sturdy ladder like she vehemently believes any practical and sensible homeowner should.

Now, in her living room, he says to her, “You know I can’t turn down an offer of Sole Soup.” His hungry eyes decide for her that supper will come before the carpentry project. After several helpings of the healing stew, as he prepares to start working, Henry offers, “Is there anything else here that needs mending? There’s a two for one special tonight,” he grins at her.

“Funny you ask,” she jumps on the opportunity to talk to a captive Henry while he is on the ladder.
Just then they hear Aaron knock and slip in the back door. “Mrs. Pingrey? Henry?”

"We're over here!"

"Sorry, I'm late." He leans back so he can see them. "Henry didn't eat all the stew did he?" He winks at Henry. Aaron puts a bag on the counter and fishes out their dessert.

"Help yourself Aaron, bring your bowl in here so we can talk while you eat," she suggests.

As Henry fixes the shelf, Mrs. Pingrey and Aaron steer the conversation to the subject of family and support systems, and dealing with difficult times.

Finally, Henry, still on the ladder, half turns towards them and says, "Alright, let's have it."

Aaron and Mrs. Pingrey eye each other with guilt. Mrs. Pingrey broke the silence, "Sorry, dear, we didn't know how to approach it. We didn't want to push you in the wrong direction."
Henry waits.

Aaron pulls out of his pocket a re-sealable plastic bag of sealed disposable syringes. "They were amongst the belongings that came from Jonathan's wreckage. They're not Jonathan's. That much we know."

They didn't bother telling Henry, that when they received the box of Jonathan's belongings from the towing company, Aaron inspected Jonathan for needle marks.

Not wanting to be confrontational, Aaron treads lightly. "Will you tell us, Henry, if you need our help? Are they yours?"

"They are mine, so to speak. Thanks for your concern, but I don't need your help. I should have told you sooner." Henry comes down from the ladder. They talk a while.

Later that evening, Henry and Aaron pick up their dessert dishes and place them in the sink. "Do you want to come join me? I can use the extra hand!" Henry invites them both as he takes the bag of syringes back from Aaron.

"Thanks, I shall. If I had known sooner, I'd have joined you sooner." Aaron grins, relieved. They all chuckle. Mrs. Pingrey decides to let the two have some time together, so she offers to stay.

"Run along, do what you need to do. I can handle this." She returns to the living room to pick up the tools. She eyes the shelf above and smiles, pleased.

Before Henry arrived, Mrs. Pingrey took a moment to assess the state of the top shelf. Then she climbed the ladder, eyed her footing, slipped and grabbed the shelf for support causing the nails to loosen.

That night, before leaving, Henry gives the shelf a shake testing the handiwork. The once precarious shelf was made sturdy once again with stronger braces. Henry comments that he had thought he braced it well enough when he put it up last month. She tells him she grabbed it when she slipped.

"It's not like you to slip," Henry says.

"No, it isn't. But that's what happened." She flashes him confident eyes.

“Hmmm,” Henry says with doubt. Then he gives her a hug before he leaves. “You are unbelievable, Mrs. P.”

Aaron winks at her over Henry's shoulder.

After they leave Mrs. Pingrey studies the pamphlet that Henry left for her. She smiles. She and Aaron needn't worry after all.

CHAPTER 3 SHATTERED

SHAMELESSLY

All through Jonathan's ups and downs, Marion remains steadfast and calm, until one day. Marion calls out to Jonathan, "Aaron's coming by to drop something off."

"When?"
"Any minute now."
"Okay."

Jonathan continues washing dishes. The washing machine hums in the background, and Marion chops vegetables. But suddenly in the middle of sounds of routine mornings, a teacup slips from Jonathan's hands and lands on the floor.

The shatter is like a shard of glass intruding on their peaceful morning. As he bends over to pick up the broken pieces, he is reminded of the night he lost Moriah. The memories flood back into him as real as the night it happened. He hears the crash, the explosion, the yelling.

Jonathan spirals into the deep again. He turns to his mother with fear of the pain that lies behind this wake. There is a tremor in his voice. "Mother," Jonathan's chest tightens. He's breathing harder and soon is overcome by an unexplained rip over his heart. He tries to tell her what's wrong.

“I feel something again. My chest, it...it feels like I’ve been run through and the blade is slicing my heart in two!” Shaking now, he tells her under his breath, “Mother, I hurt all over!”

She replies, “I know, dear. I know,” trying to console him, but as she approaches to embrace him, Jonathan suddenly turns to face her and yells in anger,

“How would you know? Nobody knows! Everyone keeps saying 'they know,' but they don’t. How could any of you know that it hurts so much that...,

...I'd rather die than feel it all over again!”

With that last remark, the sympathy that is in Marion’s eyes turn into terror. She loses herself to her pain and fear. “No! You can’t die! Not you too!” She shrieks. “Don’t you say that! Don’t you dare say it.” And she raises her hand to strike him across the face but guilt snatches her heart and her hand comes down to cover her mouth instead. “I’m sorry, I’m so sorry.” She regrets it instantly. And she turns away from him to hide her shame. “But how can I endure loss upon loss?” she mutters to herself.

But Jonathan hears her!

Jonathan just blinks. She had never displayed such pain before. Nor had she ever shown such terror, as if his uttering those words out loud would somehow dare fate. Right now, though, this very moment, it is easier for Jonathan to feel anger than to feel his own pain, and far easier to feel anger than to sense anyone else’s pain. So he chooses anger for it keeps his pain at bay. In his anger he hurls his words like blades at Marion,

“I DON’T CARE!”

She is aghast but he repeats it deliberately, and shamelessly,

"I.... DON'T....CARE!"

But worse than hearing them, Marion feels the intended harsh in his piercing words and as they found their mark, her heart bled and tears pried themselves out of her brave eyes.

UNFORGIVABLE

Aaron hears the commotion as he approaches the house and he enters with great urgency. He steps into the room just in time to hear Jonathan deliver those three unthinkable words to his mother.

"What's all this yelling about? Marion?" She wipes her cheeks, but before she could reply,

Jonathan confronts Aaron in a big voice, "What are you doing here?" He has more than enough anger to turn against Aaron, too.

Taken off guard, Aaron says, "I'm trying to help."

"Well, stop trying to help! You're not any help. Don't think I don't know what you've been doing, hovering around my mother all the time. I've seen how you look at her. I know that look! You're, you're," he stammers. Not able to think of anything to accuse him of, he blurts out, "You're planning something!"

"Look, Jonathan, you can be mean and nasty to me, and I'll let it pass, but you'll not be heartless and cruel to your mother. I'll not have it."

"What gives you the right?" Jonathan challenges, pacing in the little corner of the kitchen.

"I have every right to protect your mother, if you haven't the sense to protect her from your ugly hurtful self, right now!" Taking a moment to take a recovering breath, Aaron lowers his voice and says, "Look, there's no need for this," trying his best to remain rational. "You're pushing away the very people..." and Aaron never finishes his sentence. He makes the mistake of lowering his gaze as he rubs his forehead and Jonathan's wild angry swing makes contact with Aaron's jaw. But being twice as massive as Jonathan, Aaron suffers the blow and remains standing. "Now you've done it!" He snatches Jonathan by the collar and twists one arm behind his back while he shoves him towards the door. "Get out of here before I box your ears!"

"Who do you think you are? You can't throw me out of my own house! You don't even live here!" Jonathan rabidly protests.

"I meant 'Get out and Cool Off! Go to Henry's.' And while you're there, think about what you've said and done, and don't come back until you're ready to apologize to your mother!" With that, Aaron promptly tosses him out the front door. Jonathan, anger still in his veins, runs away in the direction of Henry's place.

"I feel like an ass." Aaron's eyes are downcast.

"You aren't an ass," Marion says.

"That didn't go well. We must've sounded like idiots."

"Jonathan sounded like an idiot. You," she thought, 'sounded like a father,' but instead she says, "You said and did the right things. Considering, it was probably the best thing. And, thank you." "Whatever for?" he grabs a bag of frozen lentils from the freezer, and Marion guides him to a chair.

"For not boxing him in the ears." She manages to smile through the tears drying on her face.

Jonathan forgets his keys to Henry's place. Now too ashamed to go back home, he walks over and knocks on Mrs. Pingrey's door. Upon seeing him standing there distraught, she exclaims, "Why, Jonathan, come in here. What's wrong?"

She quickly ushers him into the living room. Jonathan paces, too distressed to sit. "I can't ever go back home and face mother and the doctor. What I did is unforgivable! I'm an awful person. Mrs. Pingrey, what'll I do? How am I ever going to fix this?"

For as long as he could remember, Jonathan could always count on Mrs. Pingrey to help him when he couldn't sort things out himself, and to advise him when he asked for it, but today, she just kept nodding, which made him keep talking. When he had emptied out his chest, exhausted at the endeavor, he fell asleep on her soft warm cushions.

PERTURBED

Meanwhile, Henry returns to his home oblivious to the events in progress. Marion and Aaron fall asleep in their chairs waiting. Marion wakes with a start when the phone rings. She shakes Aaron's knee to wake him.

"It's Henry," she tells Aaron. "Yes, Henry?"
"I need to ask Jonathan something please. He's not answering his phone."
"I thought he was with you," exclaims Marion, not expecting this turn of events.
"No, I've been gone. I haven't talked to him all day."

She gives a summary of earlier events trying not to agitate Henry too much. She tells him about Jonathan hitting Aaron because he'd find out eventually anyway. She does, however, intentionally leave out the tiny unnecessary detail about Jonathan shouting at her. But Henry hears the slight warble in her voice which prompts him to ask her, "Did he *make you cry*?"

She didn't want to tell him the truth, but, neither did she want to lie to Henry. So instead, she simply didn't answer.

"Did he?" he asked more firmly.

"Oh, Henry, does it really matter?" Immediately, Marion and

Henry both came to the same conclusion, 'Not a good answer.' and for the same reason, 'Jonathan will have to answer to Henry for this.' Henry is done being patient now. 'Jonathan has crossed the line this time. This has got to stop,' Henry said to himself. Before he thinks of what to say to Marion, she hears the door.

"Henry, wait, I think that's him at the door now, yes."

"Keep him there! I'm coming right over!"
Henry, though furious, is able to think clearly enough to make a call before he grabs his keys.

When Jonathan raises his head from Mrs. Pingrey's cushions, he sees her dozing in a chair next to his. He decides to let her sleep and so leaves quietly to return home. Slowly, he walks in the doorway, and carefully turns towards it so he could ease it shut with no sound, thinking Marion may be asleep, and hoping she wouldn't hear him. He turns around and is surprised to meet two anxious faces.

"What have I done now?" he scowls.

"Where have you been?" Marion demands.

"As I recall, you're the ones who asked me to leave and stay away!" Jonathan exclaims, "How's a guy supposed to calm down and cool off when everybody's edgy all the time?"
Aaron and Marion look at each other and realize he is right. They are being unduly edgy.

"If you must know, I was locked out from Henry's. I was at Mrs. Pingrey's," he boasts.

SORRY ENOUGH

When Jonathan blurts out that small detail, everyone seems to calm down a bit. Finally, Jonathan eases towards his mother to hug her, and then sheepishly whispers in her ear, "I'm sorry, Mother." After a moment, he asks to talk to Aaron. Marion silently tells herself, 'I'll have to tell him someday, how proud I am of him.' She offers to make tea and moves to the kitchen so they can be alone.

Now facing Aaron squarely, Jonathan hesitates, searching for the right words. He only now realizes this is harder than he first thought. He was taught to look people in the eye when he apologizes. That was difficult enough, but to actually look at the mark he made on Aaron's face. "I'm sorry I hit you."

"Accepted." Aaron replies at once, "Mind you, under any other circumstances, you realize, I would have floored you, right?"
But, Jonathan saw a grin forming on the corner of Aaron's mouth. And this eased Jonathan's next effort at making amends.

"And all that stuff I said about you and mum, I didn't mean it. I'm really, truly sorry."

"Don't apologize for that just yet."
"What do you mean?" Jonathan didn't understand.
"You know I wouldn't hurt your mother don't you?"

"Yeah, I know."
"That said, you weren't entirely wrong." Aaron takes him aside, and with an arm over Jonathan's shoulder, Aaron peers towards the door to see that Marion wasn't near.
"I need to talk to you, and Henry, too. But not here."

They are interrupted by a suspicious jostling at the back door. It is late at night. Jonathan moves towards the door, Aaron right behind. No one should be knocking at this hour. Whoever it is, is not knocking but rather, shaking the doorknob. Little did they know that it is Henry in escalating frustration that he can't seem to unlock the *'damn'* door as Henry would put it. Jonathan opens it just as Henry withdraws his key.

"Good!" cries Henry. Then suddenly Henry barges in the house, rushes to Jonathan, grabs him by the shirt and pushes him past a dumbfounded Aaron, down onto a chair. "Don't Move!" Henry commands, and Jonathan obeys.

"Stay away from me! I'm bigger than you now!" Jonathan's voice may be threatening but his body cowers, betraying him.
Henry disappears into a large closet and reappears with a bat.

"You may be bigger, but you know that's not a problem." With the bat in one hand, Henry grabs Jonathan with the other and half drags him toward the door. "You're coming with me," he continues.

"What's going on?" Jonathan says nervously.

"Shut up!" Henry shouts at him before tossing him out into the night.

Marion hears Henry's voice, reappears, then calls out, "Henry, it's alright! He's apologized already."

“I’m sure he's not sorry enough,” Henry replies confidently.

“Do you know what you’re doing, Henry?” Aaron asks, sizing up the need for him to step in.

Henry steps back, turns to them and with a calmer voice says, “Trust me. Besides, Mrs. Pingrey knows.”

Marion's and Aaron's eyes meet and they nod at each other. They are at a loss for an explanation but they trust Henry enough to wait.

DOESN'T COMPARE

Henry urges Jonathan towards the truck, then tells him, "Get in!" Jonathan hesitates so Henry pushes him into the truck and shoves the bat into his hands. "Hold this while I drive, and NO TALKING," he says firmly.

Jonathan figures out that whatever it is Henry's got to say to him, Henry didn't want to say it in front of Marion or Aaron. What's more, Jonathan notices Henry engage the child lock just before shutting the truck door. While Henry isn't looking, Jonathan tries the door handle. He's trapped! Henry makes the tires spin as they pull away from the house.

"Where are you taking....."

Thwapp! Henry slaps him in the ears with a hat in the truck. "Don't talk!"

"I already said I was sorry," he whines.

"Not as sorry as you're going to be." Henry's voice was unnervingly calm all of a sudden.

Jonathan tries to reassure himself, 'Maybe he is concentrating on his driving. He is going unusually fast.' Then a scary thought occurs to him, "Are you going to take me to the river?" Jonathan continues with dread, and he suggests in desperation, "It's too dark to go to the river!"

Henry replies with eerie silence.

"You're scaring me!" Jonathan adds.

"You should be scared," Henry says in a very level tone. The pickup swerves this way and that.

"You know what happened the last time I was in the river, Henry!"

"Are you thick or what?" Henry's voice, now, slightly irritated. But Henry quickly regains composure and says calmly, "The river's the other way."

Now, Jonathan is really scared. He has never seen Henry so unduly unperturbed. Right now, he thought he would much prefer the over- the-top-angry Henry.

Jonathan tries a little humor. "You wouldn't happen to be in a homicidal mood would you, you know, like that one time?" His fears grow when he remembers the day he ran over Henry's motorcycle with Henry's truck.

Henry remembers, too. "This doesn't compare," Henry replies, again in a scary level tone.

"Just what are you getting at?" Jonathan's wry smile fades.

AS MUCH OR MORE

"Let's just say, you're going to wish you were dead," warns Henry.
Jonathan starts sniveling.
"What now!?" Henry's patience is running thin.
Jonathan answers with more sniveling.
"I said 'You'll WISH you were dead.' I didn't say, 'You'll BE dead."

This only encouraged Jonathan's mind to conjure up things worse than death. His unfettered imagination takes over to his dismay, and visions of torture and mayhem dominate his thoughts.
"Well I can think of a thing or two worse than death," Jonathan gasps, hoping Henry doesn't ask him for examples.

Realizing Jonathan's imagination has run amok once again, Henry says, "Really, you watch too many sick movies!" He rolls his eyes. "And STOP that SNIVELING!" Now Henry sounded like his old self, angry, but normal.

Jonathan chokes back his sniveling and sits up, shoulders hunched forward. He scoots as far away as he can. He wipes his nose on his sleeve but tries to hide it.

"Another sound out of you and you'll be sitting in the back!" Henry warns him.

Meanwhile Mrs. Pingrey is talking on the phone to a man in a gray jumpsuit.
"Don't call the police. They'll be fine. Thanks."

Henry swerves the truck into a gravel driveway of a wrecking yard at the end of town. It should be closed and dark, but it isn't. Henry parks, and yanks him out of the truck and snatches the bat from his hands. He pushes Jonathan between rows of cars to a clear area and drops the bat to the ground.

"Alright, you!" Without warning, Henry slaps him squarely in the face. "That's for being a blind idiot and an ass!"

Jonathan blinks. Henry's not fooling. That really hurt! Jonathan nurses his face with his hand.

"What do you want from me?" Jonathan whines, "I said, 'I was sorry.'" He backs away from Henry.

But Henry follows. "You have no idea! You don't even *know enough* to be really sorry!" And Henry slaps him on the other side of his face. "And that, my friend, is for treating your family like shit!"

"But that's the same thing!" Jonathan protests as he puts his arms up around his head in case Henry hits him again.

"You hit Aaron for no good reason. Don't you remember, not too long ago, you were drowning, Aaron saves your ass, and now you hit him! And you don't even realize how much you've hurt your very own mother. You can hurt as much or more with words you know. Do you even know you made her cry? You might as well have hit her, too!"

'Now that,' Jonathan thought with agony, 'That one, I deserve.'

"And you better hell not have hurt Mrs. Pingrey!"

"I didn't! I wouldn't!" He turns sideways and flinches, thinking back, wondering with fear if he might have without realizing it.

"You've no right to hurt the people who have been there for you. If you want to lash out at somebody, then why not hit me?" Henry grabs him by the shirt and shoves him. "Not them! They don't deserve it. Come on, why don't you hit me? Hunh? Hit me! Come on, tell me. Why are you being such an idiot to your family? What's your excuse?"

Now Jonathan feels really bad, turns away, and starts sniveling. Jonathan tells himself, Henry's right, words can hurt worse than being hit. Jonathan feels it right now. "I didn't mean to. I've just been," Jonathan is trying his best to stifle his emotions. He didn't want Henry to see. But realizes it's useless to hold it back. "Moriah," he sobs.

Henry knocks him over from behind and sits on him. He's pinned to the ground with his face in gravel.
"That's it? That's all you've got? That's your excuse?"

"It's not an excuse. It's a reason!" Jonathan is yelling too, now, only it's hard for him to get enough air with Henry's full weight on his lungs. "Get off me!" he gasps.

"Excuse. Reason. No difference." Henry is squashing his face into the gravel. In a very acerbic tone, Henry says, "You're telling me that you have been behaving like an idiot because of Moriah?"

"You don't understand! I love her. I miss her, and," Jonathan gasps for air. "I HURT!" His voice is that of a little boy.

Henry takes a quivering breath. With untold pain he chokes back tears and with great difficulty, musters his determination to see this through. Contrary to the pity in his eyes, he gives his voice a boastful tone, “We lost her too, you know.”

Henry leans back and loosens his grip on Jonathan, then turns away, as if to hide his face, even though Jonathan can’t possibly see it. He pauses to wipe his face on his sleeve. His face, now full of compassion, in no way reflects the anger he projects with his voice. “You hurt because you love her,” Henry declares for Jonathan.

“Yes,” Jonathan reluctantly admits, unsure of Henry's intentions.
“You *still* hurt because you *still* love her.”
“Yes!”
“Then stop loving her!” And with that, Henry shoves Jonathan’s face in again. “Give it up! If you don’t love her, you wouldn’t hurt. Say it!”
“No!”
“Say it. ’I don't love her anymore.’ SAY IT!”
“NO!”
Cruelly pressing every word into Jonathan's face with the gravel, Henry says, “I ...DON’T ...LOVE ...HER.” Then again, Henry wipes his face with his sleeve.

“NO!” Suddenly, Jonathan throws Henry off his back, sending him toppling backwards.

Free from Henry’s grip, Jonathan clambers onto his feet, and with clenched fists at his sides, Jonathan hurls his words at Henry, “I won’t stop loving her, EVER, even if it hurts until the day I die! I choose to love her forever, even if it hurts FOREVER! You can’t tell me how to feel about her! I CHOOSE TO LOVE HER!” Jonathan’s chest heaves as he catches his breath, “and even when it stops hurting, I KNOW I WILL STILL LOVE HER.”

Henry recovers and stands, panting. Finally, his voice, now more gentle, "I didn't come here to tell you how to feel about Moriah. I came here to ask you to listen to what you just told me. Just listen to your own words. Just accept it. All of it. For now, anyway. Then later, who knows?"

They both pause in thought, catching their breath. After a little while, Henry breaks the silence,

"But I do suggest one thing."
"What?" Jonathan replies.
"Tell your pain to stick its sorry head up its ass, because you're gonna love Moriah forever whether the pain is there or not."

Jonathan doesn't know what to think. He decides though, that Henry looks and sounds like Henry again. With not another word, Henry finds the bat and gives it to him, then walks over to a car behind a heap of junk in the distance. As Jonathan approaches, he sees a car that looks foreign and familiar at the same time. As Henry moves aside, Jonathan recognizes it eventually. He walks around it in a big circle, reacquainting himself with the car he once knew and depended on. It is blackened where the fire had tried to devour all of them. He sees the seat where Moriah last sat. He takes a breath, unsure.

Then Jonathan lets loose his feelings and the boldest, his anger runs through his body, permeates his chest, runs down his arms, quickly becoming fury as he feels the impact of the bat against metal and glass. After only several blows, his unbridled emotion emanates from his throat as he brings the weapon down over his head. He means to decimate the behemoth that killed his daughter. He beats the monster again and again. It has long since stopped breathing, but Jonathan continues to punish it until he is empty, no fury, no anger, no tears, no strength left. Even the pain leaves his heart for a while. All he feels now are his lungs needing air and a wretched dryness gripping his throat. He drops to the ground and leans back on the metal carcass, his own body, spent. It is difficult to tell which is worse off, the young man or the battered beast.

Henry had ducked into the office nearby, which, strangely, had its lights on. When he notices the banging stop, he emerges and comes to where Jonathan is sitting on the ground. Jonathan offers him the bat. "You wanna give it a go?" he says in a weak hoarse voice.

"No, thanks," Henry replies with grinning eyes.

Then silence. Darkness. And a terrifying monstrous noise. Then suddenly, floodlights.

The gaping jaws of a metal compactor about to swallow the remnants of the car whole, await the signal. Henry is standing next to the proprietor in front of the big machine. "May I?" gestures Henry. The proprietor motions to a big red button, which Henry presses, sending the giant maw in motion. The compactor groans as the beast resists, but eventually what is left of Jonathan's once loyal car is smashed into a small conglomeration of entangled unrecognizable metal.

"Let's go." Henry throws Jonathan's arm over his shoulder, and spills him into the truck. Jonathan collapses into the passenger's seat. Then Henry shuts the door.

NEED TO KNOW

Henry drives away weary and envious of Jonathan who drops off to sleep, but who, after a little while , opens his eyes and notices, “Hey, this isn't the way home. Aren't you taking me home?”

“Not yet,” Henry says blandly.

Jonathan sits up straight and tall, turns in his seat and faces Henry as the truck bounces along in the dark on the hilly windy road. “Look here,” Jonathan demands. “Just how much more am I supposed to take from you? You’re coming off as abusive now. I get it, Okay? I shouldn’t have taken it out on Mum and Aaron. I’ve been an ass, not to Mrs. Pingrey, though, and I’ve hurt my family. First you kidnap me, then slap me around even though I don’t fight back, and now I ache all over, and I feel nausea coming on, and...”

Henry stomps on the brakes, throwing Jonathan's face into an untimely intimate encounter with the dash of the truck.

“Awwww! Henry!” Jonathan hollers angrily, as he pushes himself back into his seat with one hand and nurses his face with the other.

“You are NOT going to throw up in my truck!” Henry points his finger Jonathan's way, “Open the door and get out!”

“I can’t you buffoon! You put on the child lock remember? Aww!” he groans, still cradling his face where it met truck.

Panicking now, Henry hollers, “Then stick your head out the window!”

Jonathan fiddles with the window button. “It’s not working!”

In desperation Henry turns off the engine, gets out, and marches over to Jonathan's side. Henry throws the door open, pulls him out and away from his truck, and points to the ground.

“You do realize there’s a difference between nausea and actual vomiting don’t you! With all those medical books you read. I said I *feel* nausea. I didn't say I was going to actually vomit!” Jonathan touches his face lightly and winces. Although it was subsiding, the pain was refusing to leave. “You abuse the child lock, forget the seatbelt, and you freak out over someone feeling nauseous in your truck! You know, you're going to make an EXCELLENT FATHER SOMEDAY!” Jonathan vents with escalating fervor.

Henry is ignoring his rant. Instead he is looking about, trying to regain his bearings in this darkness. “I swear you talk too much. Shut up, we’re here.”

“Where?” Jonathan momentarily forgets the pain in his face.

“We can enter the back way.” Henry leads the way through the bushes and over a wall.

Fortunately, there are rows of lanterns along the way.

Jonathan is grateful for the little light they have. "What are we doing here, Henry?" Jonathan whispers with growing fear.

While Henry uses his normal conversational voice, "Why are you whispering?"

"Because..." Jonathan doesn't finish his sentence. He knows his imagination will surely conjure up things worse than any confessions he may verbalize. Instead he whispers, with a tone of persuasion, "What's so important, it can't wait until daylight?"

"You'll know how important it is when you see it."

Finally, they arrive before a marker. From behind the stone, their faces are lit by a nearby lamp. A moth flutters about the light, insistent, a haunting memory that wouldn't be ignored.

Jonathan bends down for a closer look at the stone's markings. "Same names. What of it?"

"Think, man. What are the chances? In our town? Look at the dates."

Jonathan studied the stone again, and makes the calculations. "You mean..."

Henry finishes his thoughts. "She couldn't have been more than nineteen."

With profound realization of the depth of the injury he had dealt on his mother's heart, Jonathan takes a long undeserved breath. He wants to look away but something makes him look at the letters etched in the cold stone. It pained him to remember yelling at his mother, "I DON'T CARE!!" He forcibly shuts his eyes, trying to make the images go away. He opens them realizing they will not so easily be spurned.

Henry, meanwhile, remembers talking to Mrs. Pingrey earlier. "Please, Mrs. Pingrey, for Jonathan's sake, *I need to know*." She cradles the phone with both hands and slowly, carefully choosing her words, she says to him, "It is not for me to say. You must ask Marion." An invisible hand clenched Henry's throat. It was all he needed to know to decide what to do next.

Jonathan reaches for the stone to steady himself. He sighs, eyes swimming with deep regret for what he committed earlier that day, and now also, compassion for his mother for what he inflicted upon her.

"Oh, Henry, what have I done?!" To think, earlier at the junkyard, Jonathan thought that he couldn't feel much worse.

"I'm sorry, Jonathan." After some silence, Henry rises and nudges Jonathan's shoulder, "I can take you home now."

Wanting to and not wanting to go home, a decidedly torturous battle in Jonathan's mind, he surrenders to his fate and lets Henry help him back into the truck. This time, Henry remembers the seatbelt.

I UNDERSTAND NOW

In the truck on the way home, Henry clears his throat, and asks Jonathan, "Can I ask you something? Why wouldn't you hit me? Back there at the junkyard. Why wouldn't you fight me? Even when I said hurtful things? Even when I hit you?"

"You mean, even though you were trying your hardest to make me hit you? I can't hit you," he says, "I've got no cause."

"But, I thought," Henry looks confused, "Those days you weren't talking to me?"

"Those days, I don't recall talking to anybody."

"Then, you didn't blame me for what happened?"

Jonathan shakes his head, "No, never."

Henry has always had difficulty expressing his innermost feelings. Today, more so. He pulls over to the side of the road to gather his thoughts. Softly, he began to say, "I thought..."

Jonathan finishes for him. "...that she died because of something you did or didn't do, that it was your fault, and that you failed her somehow," Jonathan speaks softly, gently, as if the words cause him pain and he didn't want his words to hurt Henry. "What's more, you thought you'd hate yourself forever."

"How do you know all that?" It is as if Jonathan read his mind.

"I'm not as big an idiot as you think," Jonathan looks at him thinking, 'You can't be serious?' and says, "It's not that hard to figure out." He smiles. "Come on. Take me home, will you?"

"You're not going to tell me *how* you know are you?"

"I'll let you squirm a little." Jonathan sneaks a meek grin.

"Really, you're full of shit." Henry starts the engine. "Then at least tell me this, why don't you hit me, *ever*?"

"That one's easy. Best friends don't hit."

Henry scoffs with a grin and shakes his head. Then he pulls back into the road again, this time, not saying a word. They ride for a bit.

But Henry couldn't let the other question go. "So, how do you know what I was thinking?"

"I'll tell you at the house."

"I'll throw you in the river," Henry says quickly not even bothering with a threatening tone.

"Okay, before I tell you, think about it a moment. It'll come to you. Just put yourself in my shoes."

Henry is silent for a while. Then he gives two sideways glances. Jonathan keeps facing forward but his eyes dart over to Henry twice. Finally, Henry broke the silence. "I guess, I don't get to throw you in the river."

Marion greets Jonathan and Henry at the door. It is fortunate that Aaron is there to bandage them up. Otherwise, her motherly fears would have prompted an unnecessary trip to the emergency room. Bandages and ice are all they need. Before Aaron even finishes, they begin to fall asleep in their soft chairs. Aaron bids Marion goodnight and slips out the back door. Marion puts a blanket on Henry, who's asleep already, and kisses the top of his head. But Jonathan musters enough courage and humility to stay up.

"I am truly very sorry, Mother, for having hurt you. I shall regret it until the day I die." His lips quaked, "With three words, I broke your heart."

"Maybe just bruised it." She smiles at him. "And not three, I counted six."

Jonathan is puzzled.

"You said it twice, remember?" Marion quips.

Jonathan doesn't pick up on Marion's attempt at levity. He's in too serious a mode. "Oh, mother, my crime is twice as heavy as I thought!"

"It wasn't a crime. Just a mistake. One that I imagine will be unlikely that you'll make again."

"That's beside the point. I don't know how I can undo what I've done."

"You just did, Jonathan." And she whispers in his ear,

"I forgive you. Now, forgive yourself."

Even as he was falling asleep, Jonathan thought, 'One should be so lucky as to have a second chance to do something important right.' Marion didn't know what came over her son, but she could feel the depths of his sincerity this time. She kisses his temple and pushes his hair away from his tired face.

"Go to sleep, Pappy."
"You haven't called me that in years," he said sleepily.
"It became Moriah's special name for you remember? Not just your nickname anymore, so I let her have it, for you, my dear Papillon."
"I like hearing you say it." And he closes his eyes.

And while he was breathing softly, Marion whispered, "I like saying it."

Without opening his eyes, Jonathan mutters, "Mum? Remember what we talked about at the birthday party? You know, about Henry?"

Marion's gaze looks far away. That night seems a world apart from this one. "Yes, I remember."

Before falling fast asleep, Jonathan manages to say,

"I understand now. It's okay."

CHAPTER 4 MY TURN

NOT HERE!

The following morning, Marion is up early. She has a lot of catching up to do, so she starts the wash. That always seems a good place to start. She was starting to tidy up when she remembered Henry is here. 'Now, where did I stash his clothes from the other day again?' She asks herself.

Meanwhile, upstairs, Henry is up as well. He has to get to work in a hurry, even if his body does ache for more sleep. Marion slips into Moriah's room to put away some photographs and as she exits, she inadvertently leaves the door slightly open. She goes to Henry who's near the bathroom down the hall and brings him the towel and clothes she found.

"No shirt. You'll have to borrow one of Jonathan's."

"I'll still have to go home to get into my uniform. Sorry, I can't help with breakfast. I'll be late for work."

She touches his face to get a good look into his eyes. "Are you alright?"

"Yeah." He looks away. "I'm good. I could use some sleep though. Not something I usually say when I've just gotten up."

He turns to her again, and manages a weak smile.

"Come for dinner tonight. You'll be too tired to cook. Let me cook for you, then stay."

"I will. I'd like that very much." He kisses her on the face.

Then Marion gives him a comforting embrace, that he knew only she could give. He cherishes these moments. He gives her another quick kiss on her cheek. "Gotta go," and ducks into the bathroom.

She heads downstairs to put on some housework music. Henry, remembering the shirt, turns to Jonathan's closet. He's not surprised to find two of his shirts. One in particular is his favorite. He felt an urge to trounce Jonathan in his sleep, but thought twice. 'Not today,' Henry tells himself. As he turns into the hallway he notices that Moriah's door is ajar.

Without thinking much about it, he grabs the knob to pull it shut, but then hesitates, then peeks in. It has been such a long time since he had last seen the inside. He places his shirt on the floor just outside the doorway, and enters carefully, not knowing why he is drawn inside. He's uncertain why his hand reaches out to touch things. Slowly he looks around and notices Teddy on the chair. He takes Teddy, first with one hand, sits on his heels, then holds Teddy before him with both hands. Henry starts to tear, but swallows it back. He shuts his eyes for what seems an instant, but when he opens them, he sees that he has Teddy in his clutches so tight, Teddy would have cried out in terror if he were alive.

Something is happening inside him. He can feel it. He recognizes the feeling, and he has quelled it before, but this time is different.

A silent rumbling is building up like a quake that can't be heard because it lies too deep within the earth. And right behind the quake, he feels a hot flowing river of molten rock, pulsing its way out from the deep, seeking to escape. Henry can no longer hold the monster down. He doesn't have the strength to keep this wretched creature imprisoned. Henry is terrified of what might be let loose if it were to escape to the surface. The walls behind the gates are slowly filling with its massive form. Now it is challenging the gates. It is demanding to be set free.

Henry thought, 'He mustn't let it, not here!' Not with Marion and Jonathan so close, and Mrs.Pingrey is sure to rush over if she heard. So Henry dashes out. His mind's a jumble. Where are my keys? He tells himself, 'Gotta get out of here! It mustn't happen here! He needs to get away from them!'

Marion only gets a glimpse of Henry's face when he darts past her near the door. Marion senses something is wrong. "Where are you going?"

STRONG ENOUGH

He is afraid to speak, afraid the gates would burst open. Henry doesn't remember answering. But, apparently, Marion hears Henry say, "The bridge." But before she could say anything, Henry goes out the door and drives away. She runs upstairs, calling, "Jonathan! Jonathan!" She meets him in the hallway. They both turn to see Moriah's door wide open and Teddy on the floor where Henry abandoned him.

"He's run off to some bridge. It's not good."
"Mother, which bridge?"
"He didn't say." Her eyes reflect her helplessness. So Jonathan and Marion split up. Jonathan grabs the keys to the car.

Henry drives deliberately, his training working to his advantage. It seems his fears subside soon after he is a fair distance from the house. The knowledge that he is away from them calms him slightly. He reaches the bridge without incident. Jonathan is going on a hunch, because of something Henry said about a bridge the night before, but Jonathan was half asleep, and couldn't remember what it was that Henry said. Jonathan is not far behind.

Henry pulls over abruptly at the foot of the bridge. His agitation returns by the time he stomps over to the middle of the bridge, where the river is deepest. He knows when his emotions erupt, it will consume him, but now he doesn't care anymore. He grabs the wall in defiance and kicks it and screams repeatedly. The raging waterfall swallows up his voice into insignificance.

As Jonathan pulls up alongside Henry's truck, he sees Henry but doesn't hear him. Henry is pacing to and fro with his hands to his head. Jonathan fears for Henry his emotional state and his state of mind. This is not a good place for Henry to be, standing so precariously near opportunity. Jonathan has a gnawing, growing awareness of what he must do if Henry makes an unwise move. Still, Jonathan is more and more uncertain if he's strong enough for both of them. He must say or do something to steer Henry away from here or else, they could both perish. The last time Jonathan was in churning waters, Jonathan feared it would be his last. Now, his fear tempts him to look into the roaring torrent below, but fear for Henry makes him keep his eyes on Henry instead. He inches towards Henry.

Now that he is closer, he could hear Henry's intermittent screaming. By now Henry's voice is getting hoarse. He is hunched over, not knowing what to do with his hands, breathing hard, and pacing erratically as if lost. Now and then, he would put both hands to the wall and lean forward as if to look into the water. Then he would push himself away brusquely, and pace again. But, when Jonathan was close enough for Henry to notice, Henry put up a hand to gesture Jonathan to stop where he stood.

"That's why I came here," he explained, "to be away from the house. I didn't want it to happen there. I was afraid to hurt somebody. I didn't want anyone to see me do this." He starts to whimper and his body droops as he turns away slightly, ashamed of his face. Snatching the opportunity, Jonathan lunges forward and traps Henry in his arms.

"NO! You don't understand! I want to break something, hit somebody! I might hurt you! I don't want to hurt you!" As Henry wrestles against Jonathan's hold, they both lose their balance and fall to the ground. Henry again tries to wriggle free but Jonathan is hanging on for dear life, Henry's and his. Henry panting, says, "I must not hurt you," his voice less hostile. "I can't hit you. Remember what you said last night?" he said, reminding Jonathan of his own soft admonitions the night before.

"It's alright, Henry. It's alright." Jonathan is trying to slow his breathing down, to paint a picture of calm for Henry.

Henry wriggles. He can't get his arms free. At first frustrated, he surrenders. 'It's just as well,' he thinks to himself. He is content in laying right there knowing he couldn't hurt Jonathan. He relaxes a little and he lets go of the anger. And as he does this, waves of opportunistic sadness comes, then a tumultuous torrent to besiege his heart. He starts to weep. Henry's only defense is to take up his anger again, so he starts screaming and kicking again. Jonathan, thankful he kept a hold, tightens his grip again.

"I can't take this anymore." Henry blurts out, "I can't live like this. I've tried. I don't know how I could've lasted this long. I can't do it. I can't keep hiding this from everyone anymore."

"Henry, just slow down, talk me through this, tell me what you mean."

"You'll hate me when I tell you everything."

"No, I won't. I can't hate you."

"STOP THAT! I HATE MYSELF!" Henry yells out, "It makes it worse when you say that."

"Alright, okay. Just tell me what you want me to know."

Henry whimpers, "I didn't get to her in time. I couldn't keep her from dying. Jonathan, I couldn't save her. I tried. I did everything I could."

"I know you tried. I was there. I was there!"

Disgusted with himself, Henry blurts out, "But it wasn't enough! I wasn't strong enough! How can it be? I've saved others, but I couldn't save *her*. I was supposed to protect her. I promised. I broke my promise. Jonathan, I'm sorry. I killed her."

"No, Henry, that's not the same thing."

"You don't remember? That day, I sat in her seat. She sat in mine. I should have died, not her.

I'm supposed to be dead!"

WE BOTH PROMISED

"But that's not true. You got us all out. If you hadn't, we could've all died in the fire."

Henry shakes his head fighting to disagree. The monster that he feared has claimed his heart and has commanded him not to believe.

"I'm supposed to be able to fix this. I can't. I can't make it stop."

"What do you want to stop?"

"I want to stop hurting inside."

"I'm sorry Henry. I thought you had let it go. I thought you were better off than I was. I didn't realize. I didn't know this is how you feel."

"It doesn't matter what I feel. I've no right to complain. I just want it to stop. I can't imagine how much worse it is for you. She is yours. I have no right to feel the way I do."

Jonathan reminds Henry, "You have every right to feel the way you do about losing her. You of all people have a right.

I was here remember, when you made the promise every year, when we both promised."

Henry remembers last year in particular, for Moriah's birthday, the three of them were on the bridge and Jonathan rises from his knee as Henry gets on his knee facing Moriah.

"You are my world. You are my Moriah," Henry said to her as he held her hand.

"I love you," she says as she wraps her tiny arms around Henry's neck.

Henry slips a bracelet onto her wrist right next to one from Jonathan, similar but different color. Moriah is wearing a fairy crown and touches a butterfly wand to Henry's shoulder, left, right, left.

"And you are my Henry."

She turns, and skips, this way and that, down to the end of the bridge to where Marion and the others were waiting.

"How long do you think she'll have the crown?" Henry watches Moriah skipping away.

"We'd be lucky to have it in one piece to take home today." They both laugh.

"And the bracelets?" Henry asks.

Jonathan pulls a plastic bag full of identical bracelets out of his pocket. "I like to plan ahead."

“Same place, same time next year then?” Henry suggests as they walk across the bridge.

“Close to her birthday, and as close to what we've been doing all these years, is good, I think.”

“Good idea, the bag of bracelets. Hey, when she’s older, we can get her real ones made of gold!”

“Yeah, that would be excellent.” They both smile contentedly.

I STILL HURT

Jonathan tells Henry in a calmer voice, "If you promise to lie still, I'll let you go."
Henry nods. They both sit up, leaning on each other.
"I'm tired of this. I can't fight it anymore. I don't have anything left." Henry replies. His face is one of total submission.
"Whatever it is I need, I don't have it in me. And I don't know where to find it."

"What about all that stuff you said to me yesterday? Why should I believe you if you don't believe yourself?" Jonathan replies.

"I believed everything I said to you. I know you lost her, and I lost her. That part's the same. So much is different. I'm sorry I took her away from you. I can't get past the feeling that *she's gone because of me*." Just saying these words is difficult on Henry's lips. He's speaking softly now, his energy and spirit ebbing, feeling every inch, a man mortally wounded.

Jonathan feels a flood of all the terrible emotions of the past weeks invade his tender battered heart. It insidiously wants to seep through every vessel in his body. For an instant he is close to succumbing to them again. Like Henry, he feels his monster fighting to get out.

Then he realizes something. “But I don’t blame you, Henry. Alright, if you must hear it, I forgive you. Do you believe me?” Jonathan implored him, “Just believe me. I never blamed you. It wasn't your fault. I don't blame you.”

“I know that you don’t. I believe you mean what you say. But, I can’t explain it, it still hurts. Maybe I don’t deserve any better.” He turns his body away from Jonathan as if to say, “Just let me suffer alone.”

Jonathan resists, “Henry, No! Don’t give up,” and clings to Henry's arm, “Henry, Don’t do this. Don't turn away from me. Don’t turn me away. *I still hurt.”*

Henry doesn’t answer. He is tired of thinking, of struggling, of wrestling against his monsters. Henry is overcome. He removes Jonathan’s hand from his arm, and brings his knees closer to his chest. Henry turns his gaze far away. And then with a pained look, closes his eyes to the world.

He wants to just be left in peace. He opened his eyes only long enough to say, “Please, just leave me.”

Henry couldn't feel any more defeated than at this moment, or Jonathan feel any more helpless. Jonathan, at that moment, gets a glimpse of the torment that weighs on Henry’s heart and his own becomes heavier for it.

He can find no words of comfort to fill the silent void between them, so instead of imprisoning Henry in his arms as he did earlier, he puts his arms around Henry to protect him from the pain and squeezes. And as he squeezes, his own heart is squeezed and tears come to his face.

Jonathan and Henry sit in the stillness in silence, his arms around Henry's drooping shoulders.

Breathing slower now, Henry, with eyes still closed starts to shiver. The few minutes they had been sitting there at the base of the cascade, the waterfalls had laid a veil of mist on their skin. Meanwhile, as a butterfly fluttered over them, with the little strength he had left, Henry let out a trembling sigh, “Moriah.”

Moriah's name floated on the mist like the butterfly for a while and then gently rested on Jonathan's heart, and he realized at that moment what may help release them from their torment. Jonathan bends down closer to Henry and urgently whispers, “I think I know what you need Henry, what we both need.

I think I know what we have to do.” As Jonathan speaks into Henry's ear, the voice of the waterfall descends upon their shoulders, casting a shroud over his words and banishing them into secrecy from the world. It was but an idea, a wisp of a memory, but like a droplet in the wind, summoned repeatedly over time, has the power to move mountains.

Henry unlocks the gates to his heart and opens his eyes, his mind blinking itself into focus. After an eternally long moment, Henry nods and asks, “How do I do it?”
“You mean, 'How do *we* do it?'” Jonathan replies.

Pausing to think first, Jonathan rises to his feet. His face a little brighter now, he cries out loud over the voice of the water, “Well,...*maybe a little every day*?” With a smile, he reaches his hand towards Henry, who reaches up and grasps it, and he pulls Henry to his feet.

Then as they walk back to the truck, Jonathan remembers what Henry said last night about the bridge. Henry at the steering wheel, on the ride home, confesses as Jonathan drifted off to sleep, "This may sound strange, but most of the time, just sitting there for a while, by the waterfalls," he pauses, "I can't explain it, but I feel better afterwards."

With Henry's arm over Jonathan's shoulder, the shivering pair make their way along the bridge. Aaron and Marion are relieved to see them as they approach on motorcycle. They had gone to the other bridge looking for Henry. As Marion helps Henry into her car, Aaron puts his arm over Jonathan's shoulder and they walk towards the truck.

"Is there anything we can do?" Aaron offers.
"I think he's starting to be better. Starting, anyway."
Aaron nods.

CHAPTER 5 MY HEART BLEEDS

SURPRISE

Jonathan discovers among the pieces of mail, an announcement of a poetry reading engagement in the big city, and Mrs. Pingrey is listed as a performer. "Newcomer," it says. Jonathan and Henry have a conversation about why she didn't invite anybody. "She has been out of sorts lately, not herself. Maybe she just plumb forgot." Marion and Aaron had other commitments and Henry gets a call to work. Jonathan decides to surprise her by coming to hear her read. He is running late. "She is probably already there," he says to Henry, who is really disappointed at missing it. Jonathan dresses up in his finer clothes, and he takes the long drive to her performance. He arrives there too late to greet her but in time to listen to one poem just before hers. The lights remain dim over the audience. She is introduced, "Lost But Not Forgotten" Written Anonymously and Read by Wynefred Pingrey.

Lost But Not Forgotten

I shall never have cried enough for lives that never were.
This one's essence, stolen some years after birth.
Now this, her life, what's left, what is it worth?
To never live the life that was meant to be hers.

Even after all these years, she cries, Tell me why!
What's the purpose of my life?
Wandering this universe, lost, this poor child,
Such is my fate, forever, for to cry.

Was it coincidence that thrice she almost died?
Once in water, once on land, and once near the sky.
Her upturned face asking for elusive answers, denied.
Shall I just live without purpose, and without purpose, die?

If I had only known this was her fate,
I would have done anything to help her escape.
She would not have been there for him to take,
I would have removed her from death's wake.

I would have hidden her from his sight,
And stood between her and her fright.
I would have protected her with all my might,
To save her from being lost, this lone child.

I would have put my arms around her little head,
And screamed, "Stay away from her. Face me instead!"
I would have taken her hand and with her fled,
Then for the rest of her life, her heart wouldn't have bled.

I was powerless to protect her or steal her away.
I didn't, couldn't, "But, why not?" you say,
Any able person would think of every way,
Possible, to save her from that fateful day.

I would've been helpless, Even if I'd been told,
I would have been powerless, Had I known,

I would have been unable to understand,
The danger that lurked, and was at hand.

I didn't, I couldn't, protect her you see,
It was impossible, I couldn't stand between,
This child and the hands of cruelty.
Lost but Not Forgotten, her essence, still, I seek.

Suddenly, Jonathan sneezes. He is rather embarrassed. Feeling another tickle, he reaches for a napkin, and sneezes again. Poor Mrs. Pingrey. Jonathan could tell her rhythm is put off ever so slightly. But he hopes no one else notices. 'Perhaps they'll think the pause is intentional,' he consoles himself.

I didn't, I couldn't, protect her you see,
No possible way I could stand between
Her and the hands of cruelty.

Remember me, was her final plea.

The forgiving audience applauds warmly. Jonathan moves towards the side of the stage to meet her and she seems outwardly surprised to see him there. He expects as much. There is an awkward moment for her as she spies his hands for a program. In his rush, he left it at his table.

'There is none. Good,' she thought to herself.

As thoughtful as ever, he had earlier picked her flowers from her own garden but wrapped it nicely and tied it with a bow. He gives her a kiss on each cheek, and presents the bouquet. Ill at ease at first, now she is all of calmness. 'It is Jonathan, after all,' she tells herself.

"Good evening, Mrs. Pingrey."

"Oh, Jonathan! Good evening! Your countenance shines like the sun, warming my heart with blessed bliss."

Jonathan doesn't know what to say in reply. He is still thinking about her poem. Instead he offers her his arm and leads her through the crowd.

"If I could choose a face, any face, that I would rather see right now, I would choose yours. Did you get all dressed up for me?"

"Anything for you, Mrs. P. By the way, you look lovely in that old thing!"

"What?!" She is surprised but not offended. This is Jonathan talking. There must be a reason. "Alright, you've got me, will you favor me an explanation?"

"Well, whenever I say, 'You look lovely,' you always say, 'What, this old thing!' So I figured I'd change it up a bit."

She laughs lightheartedly. "You always make me laugh! That's better than a compliment, any day."

"What would you like to do? Where would you like to go? Anywhere. Name it! I will make this your special night." He takes her by both shoulders and under his breath he adds, "And only because I know you're thinking about it, I got paid yesterday."

"How about Chinese?" she suggests with a gleam in her eye.

"Done! Do you have a preference?"

"I know of a place, and it's this particular little town's secret. The chef there is magnificent! Before I tell you, will you promise, there, and nowhere else?"

"I promise," he replies with a big shiny smile.

The wok is sizzling and the chef's hand raises it and pours the stir fry delight onto a platter, and brings it to a divinely set table where Mrs. Pingrey waits with anticipation. She is pleased as much with him as with herself for hoodwinking him into taking her home where he deftly made her favorite Chinese dish upon her request. Only, she calls it Pappy's Tofu Surprise.
"*Madame, Vous Tofu Surprise*!"
"Thank you kindly, Chef Jonathan Papillon."
She loves saying his middle name. It's so French! "What's the surprise ingredient?"
"Taste it and tell me what it is."
"Mmm. Do I taste something crunchy?"
"I put nuts. Like it?"
"It is an epicurean delight!" Mrs. Pingrey savors every bite.

Fortunately, over the years he took to her coaching well, because his first attempts were quite toxic. He learned early on, the difference between a tablespoon of soy sauce and a cup of soy sauce.

MY HEART BLEEDS

When they are done eating, they sit over cups of tea. Mrs. Pingrey falls into their usual banter of creative words. And Jonathan apologizes, his brain seems to be on neutral this evening.

"Not tonight, Mrs. P., please?"
"Of course, you look tired."
He looks at her in silence. She looks at him more intently.
"I'm sorry Jonathan, you're not tired. There's something wrong. What is it? Tell me."
"I don't want to spoil the evening."
"Tell me what it is and I'll tell you if it will. Agreed?"
"Can you tell me why you changed the ending of the poem?"
"How did you know?" she answers nonchalantly without actually answering the question.
"I didn't. I just suspected, and you just confirmed." He looked downward into his cup, embarrassed at his cleverness.
"What made you suspect?"
"It didn't fit. It felt like you were about to reveal why the author couldn't help her and then you said something entirely different."
"Very perceptive of you. What else did you suspect?" she averts her eyes.

"That the events are very real to the author."
"Yes."
"I would have felt the same way as the author did."
"In what way?"
"I would have done everything I could to save her, and put things right. My heart bleeds for her and the little girl."

Mrs. Pingrey's eyes soften. "You have a kindness about you that is unsurpassed, Jonathan."
"Can I ask you, what was the original ending?"

"Perhaps I'll have the author tell you herself one day." She stalls to avoid answering him directly without lying.
"She wouldn't find it intrusive of me to ask?"
"It's all in the timing."
"I would be honored to meet her."
"Right, then, do you feel better?"
Jonathan grins widely. Something about the poem bothered him earlier, but he wasn't sure exactly why. Now, he is much relieved.

Mrs. Pingrey ushers him home, "Thank you for spending your evening with me tonight. I couldn't have imagined it to be more special. You have always been one to come through with your promises. Oh, look at the time. You have work in a few hours. You need to get some sleep." They hug and bid goodnight. Then Jonathan exits through the kitchen door as usual and makes for the house. Mrs. Pingrey picks up the teacups and takes them to the sink, but her hands begin to shake, the cup and saucer rattle, and her eyes well up. She feels a grab around her throat. She quickly puts the saucer down.

'After all these years, it happens now,' she thinks to herself.

SAFE WITH ME

Meanwhile, before he reaches the house, Jonathan realizes it's a bit brisk out, and that he has forgotten his coat on the chair at Mrs. Pingrey's. He turns around to retrieve it and that's when he sees her, through the kitchen window. Something is wrong. It looks like she has her hand to her face. And she's trying to steady herself with her other hand on the edge of the sink. He rushes inside.

But by the time he gets to her she has sat on the floor, facing the cabinets.

"Mrs. Pingrey! What's wrong? Are you hurt? Did you fall, or faint? Shall I fetch Henry? Anybody?"

She shakes her head, "No," to all these queries. He tries to turn her shoulders, but she doesn't let him.

"Tell me what to do. Tell me what's wrong!"

She shakes her head, 'No,' as she tightens her fist over her chest. Jonathan can't think of what to do, so he sits on the floor next to her for a while. Then he whispers,

"Mrs. Pingrey, it's me, remember? You told me not long ago, 'To help a friend is a privilege.' Please, let me help you. How do I make things better?"

Still, she shakes her head, refusing to turn to face him.
Finally, he just speaks what is in his heart. "You're safe with me. You can let me hold you. You can cry on me if you want to. You can say everything you need to say, or you can say absolutely nothing, or anything in between. You will still be safe with me."

She makes no sound but her other hand moves to cover her mouth. He sees some tears welling in the corner of her eye. He tries to hold her. But she wouldn't turn towards him. Jonathan forces himself to think, 'What would bring this about? It has to be something big!' And he wishes he was wrong when he discovers what he had feared earlier. He blurts out, "It's the poem!...The author...It's...." And without turning around, Mrs. Pingrey reaches out a hand to clutch his sleeve. He couldn't bear to ask her out loud. Suddenly, he knew. Jonathan felt an immense gloom descend upon his heart.

He trembles as he speaks, fighting the wretched sadness that is overcoming him, "If I had been there, I would have looked for her until I found her. I would have spirited her away, taken her somewhere safe. I would have defended and protected her even unto my last breath. I would not have let anything happen to her, not while I still stand. What happened was wrong, unconscionable. If I had the power I would have prevented it from happening. I would have done all that I could. Mrs. Pingrey, I am so sorry this ever happened. It shouldn't have. It shouldn't have. If I could, I would undo it all."

Upon hearing his heartfelt pledge, she turns towards him and he is able to put his arms around her. Mrs. Pingrey's shoulders shake but nothing, no sound comes. But her eyes are of such infinite sorrow, that even the stars of the universe would dim if they saw it. She could not let anyone see, so she shut her eyes, but it isn't enough, she could feel it emanate through her eyelids. She couldn't let the world see what is flooding through, so she covers her closed eyes with one hand. Still it is not enough to hide what has been released. So, she brings her other hand up to cover the first. And her shoulders shake some more, though no sound comes forth from her distorted open mouth. And sometimes her crying ebbs, and sometimes it flows. But always she hides her eyes from him and from the world with both hands, and still, she makes no sound.

YOU ALREADY HAVE

Jonathan waits patiently with his arms around Mrs. Pingrey in silence until she shook no more. When she was ready, she brought her hands down from her eyes. He reaches into a nearby drawer and retrieves a dishtowel for her. She uses it to dry her eyes and dab her nose. Then she starts to laugh, lightly. "It's too big a job for a small hanky, isn't it?"

He chuckles softly. He knows without asking that she is better now, but he asks anyway, "Better?"

"Much. I must have scared you."

"Given the times I have scared you, I'd say you still have some catching up to do." And now they both laugh.

"You, Pappy, have a kind heart. Everyone should be so fortunate as to have a friend like you to turn to."

"The honor is all mine Mrs. P."

They sit on the floor in silence for a while, absorbing what has happened this evening.

"I didn't mean to pry. Me asking all those questions, that's what upset you."

"Shush, don't even think to apologize, Jonathan. Some things, we make happen. Some things just happen. I'm just glad you're the one here while it's happening."

'While it's happening?' Jonathan realizes, 'Then there's more!'

"Hmm. But wait, I have to splash some water on my face," she says abruptly.

She picks herself up off the floor before Jonathan realizes, and she helps him up with surprising ease. While she is gone, his eyes wander to the kitchen counter where there is a pamphlet tucked under her keys. It is the program for that evening's show. "Darn!" He realizes that he left his. Then curiosity gets the best of him and he reaches over, flips to the page to see the end of Mrs. Pingrey's poem. There, the last line, all of eight words. The first four words strike his bones like an axe hitting a tree making its leaves tremble. He reads, *"Because I was there."* Jonathan's breathing skips. His eyes flutter to where he had last seen Mrs. Pingrey, towards the hallway to the bathroom. He thinks he may have stumbled on a secret too private for his eyes. He shouldn't have touched the program! But there is *more.* Slowly his eyes move across the following four final words. It makes his heart drop. After a long moment, he sucks air into his lungs. He had forgotten to breathe! He has to hold the counter to steady himself. He is starting to tear but he could hear Mrs. Pingrey about to return. He hurriedly returns the program to the counter under her keys, and splashes water on his face, and uses a kitchen towel to dry off, with a second to spare to regain his composure. He can't let her sense that anything has changed in him from the time she left him.

Jonathan is relieved that upon her return, she decides more tea would be in order. She turns towards a kettle on the stove, and she pours for them, then they settle into some chairs. Momentarily, she suggests he really needs to get home and catch some sleep. He senses she is still out of sorts, so he stalls, makes excuses, and prolongs the conversation until soon, they see the sun peeking through the window and hear the birds greeting it. Jonathan feels better and he is quite content that Mrs. Pingrey, sounds much better as well.

To be certain, Jonathan asks her, "Are you alright?"

To which she smiles and replies, "I am."

"Will you be alright?"

And with a confident voice, she says, "I shall be."

With all willingness and sincerity, Jonathan's boundless kindness prompts him to offer just once more, "Is there anything I can do to make things better?"

Her eyes seem to say, 'Pappy, you don't realize.' Then she says to him, "You already have, my Pappy."

Later that day, Mrs. Pingrey opens her heart to a friend, and begins to write:

Would that we knew how and when our heartfelt words can touch another person in ways that would change their world....

The little girl was there at the park, near a river. There were people milling about, some sitting on blankets. They were sunning themselves, picnicking, laughing. Somehow this little girl escaped notice. She looked too small to be by herself, but she was alone. But she wasn't meandering, she walked a straight line, parallel to the river, through the crowd, but towards this tall man in the distance, his back towards her. But before she reached him, another man behind her called out her name. She didn't turn her head, she only walked faster, almost running. When he yelled her name, she ran, and the man in the distance, hearing the name, turned in her direction, smiled, and ran towards her. Just as she reached him, he put his hands on her shoulders, and she turned to face the man who was behind her.

Man following her: "There you are, come on, let's head on back."

She inched closer to the man who was holding her shoulders, and clung to his clothes. Just then a man in uniform happened by.

Park ranger: "Hello folks, can I help here?"

The two men eyed each other but before anyone could speak, the little girl spoke up and said as she took a hand from her shoulder and clung to it with both of hers.

Little Girl: "This is my Pappy."

Park ranger: "Well then," the officer said, and he turned to face the man who had called out her name but he had already disappeared into the crowd.

Pappy: "Good day, officer."

The officer bowed and went away looking for the other man to ask him questions.

And the little girl and Pappy continued to walk along the river away from the people. Pretty soon, he lifted her up and carried her in his strong arms. She had her little arms around his neck. She was looking back behind him, where they had just come from. And she turned so she could see forward, where they were going, instead. After a little while, Pappy looked into her face and asked,

"Are you alright?"

Mrs. Pingrey pauses then puts down her pen.

CHAPTER 6 RESCUING

ASKS FOR HELP

At dusk at the house, Marion picks up a call. It is Aaron. He tells Marion that he needs Jonathan's help, but he didn't say why. Marion gives the phone to Jonathan.

"Hello, what's up doctor?"
"I need to talk to you and Henry. It's better here than there. I've been meaning to for a long time. But anyway, can you and Henry come here?"
"Sure, I'll tell Henry. How about in a half an hour?"
"I told your mother I need your help, which is more or less true. You understand, right?"
"Yeah, yeah, I gotcha, no worries."

Henry and Jonathan drive up to Aaron's ranch wondering about Aaron's request, not so much that he is asking for help, which he has often done before, but more, the way he asked them to come over.

When the boys arrive, Aaron meets them just outside of the main house and asks them to bring one last horse into the barn. "This thunderstorm rolled in rather quickly. I'd be glad for some help. Then we can talk in the den," he says.

SHOULDERS A GREAT BURDEN

Henry and Jonathan try to lead one last horse indoors from the thunderstorm. Jonathan is on bareback rubbing her neck, and murmuring to her, while Henry is leading her by the reins, when suddenly blue lightning strikes nearby. She rears, tossing Jonathan backwards.

"Jonathan! Look out!"
"Henry! Look out!"

They each call out a warning to the other simultaneously. Jonathan lands hard on his shoulder but hit his head too. He is unconscious. Henry ducks but the horse lands a hoof on his back. It knocks the wind out of him but he recovers and is on his feet immediately. He scrambles to Jonathan's side who is just laying there in the rain. Henry, not thinking straight, takes Jonathan by the shoulders and shakes him. "Jonathan, are you alright? Jonathan, Jonathan!" Henry yells louder and louder.

While stunned, Jonathan doesn't sense anything around him. He wakes, then he sees, hears, and feels everything, the lightning, the rain, and the pain that stabs his shoulder.

"HENRY, STOP! LET GO! You're hurting me!"

Looking up to the sky, Henry sizes up their situation.

To Henry's dismay, there is no choice but to move him. They need to get indoors. First he grabs Jonathan's legs and drags him into the barn out of danger. All he could do is keep saying, "I'm sorry, I'm sorry." Inside the barn, Henry tries to call Aaron but fails to get through. Looking around, he spots a blanket and throws it on Jonathan. Henry is oblivious of his own injury. Jonathan who is in anguish and increasingly frightened is clutching his arm.

"Henry!" he gasps.

"Something's wrong, I've called Aaron twice. He doesn't answer. I have to run to the house to fetch him." Aaron's phone rings on the bathroom counter. Aaron, in the shower doesn't hear it, and is oblivious to their plight.

"NO! Don't leave me."

Henry reassures him, "I'll be right back, I promise."

"Henry, don't go!"

"Just hang on. It'll be OK. I need to get help."

"No!"

"I'll be quick."

Henry dashes for the main house and runs through the rain and lightning.

Just as Henry leaves, Jonathan's head swims. He hears the lightning stab the dark sky mercilessly, as his own body is stabbed by an invisible knife. Alone and frightened, he takes short shallow breaths and finds welcome solace. He knows now that to elude pain he must try to move as little as possible. But he has breathe! He shuts his eyes, wishing the pain away, but no! In the dark, the monster is bigger. When he opens his eyes again, Moriah is there before him. She takes his face in her two little hands, touches her head to his, closes her eyes, then whispers, "I'm here, Pappy."

After searching everywhere, finally, upstairs, in the main house, Henry finds Aaron. Between gasps he says, "Come quick. Jonathan,...fell off horse,...hit his head,...he's come to now, but bad pain in the shoulder, real bad."

Almost immediately, Aaron is halfway out the door with his bag. As Henry makes to follow him, Aaron sends him back to the house and orders him, "No, stay and use the radio to call for help. The bridge is out. You'll have to ask Mr. Selene to come. It's the only way!"

Aaron barges in through the barn door. For a brief moment, through the doorway, Jonathan sees the fierce lightning pierce the night sky.

"Where's Henry?" Jonathan starts sobbing, "He promised." His voice was that of an abandoned child.

Aaron's hands begin to shake because he suspects the ordeal in store for Jonathan, but he manages to speak in his soothing voice. "Henry's calling for help on the radio. He'll be here soon. Don't worry."

Aaron approaches and sits on his heels. His hands reach forward toward Jonathan who wails, afraid of the pain that is delivered by helpful hands, like Henry's only moments ago. Jonathan knows too well the price of even a little movement.

"No! NO!" Jonathan commands Aaron to stay away, then his fearsome face melts and he begs Aaron,
"Please, don't. I can't, no more, please," his face in anguish. Then he cries out, "Aaron, I'm dying!"

"Oh, no, no, Jonathan. Listen to me, you're not dying."

Accepting his undeniable fate, Jonathan explains, so Aaron would understand,

"I saw Moriah, just now. I saw her. She was here!"

Aaron had to think for a moment. Now he understands Jonathan's frightful cry.

"It doesn't mean you're dying. Moriah is here to be by your side. Do you understand? Not to take you away."

"Okay," Jonathan says in a moment of sweet surrender. Aaron's reassurance, like balm on a burn, soothed his quaking soul. Sighing, he let his eyelids close slowly, savoring Aaron's words. But another spasm of his shoulder muscles claims him and he cries out in protest, "Why won't it stop?!" As he feels another bout growing, gripping his body, wringing it into submission, tentacles of fear wrap around his heart slowly squeezing from it the little hope and courage he had left. "Aaron!" he cries out with eyes of terror, desperately clutching Aaron's sleeve and through gritted teeth he whimpers, "Aaron."

"Will you let me make things better?" Aaron says softly as he puts his hand on Jonathan's forehead, and he whispers gently,

"Son, do you trust me?"

Jonathan nods, "Yes."

As Aaron coaches him through the shards of pain he says soothingly, "Breathe, just let it in. Don't fight it. Now exhale slowly, and let it leave."

Henry returns, out of breath, but in time to help. As Aaron shows him what to do, he tells Aaron the news, "The bridge is still flooded over. They can't send an ambulance across. The lightning storm isn't any help. Mr. Selene promises to come as soon as he thinks it's safe."

During Jonathan's ordeal, he unwittingly uses some exquisitely elaborate expletives which Aaron has only ever heard Henry use. And he managed to kick Henry three different occasions, which Henry paid for dearly. There were times Henry doubted he could take much more himself. But even now Henry knows, he'd much rather a kick in the ribs over the feeling that came over him when Jonathan's body suddenly went limp and lifeless in his arms. Aaron was concentrating on manipulating the shoulder, and remained silent, pausing only to slap Jonathan lightly on the cheek, "Jonathan, Jonathan." When Jonathan didn't respond, Aaron resumed what he was doing. He didn't realize that in that short moment, Henry's world had capsized.

As an unseen wind sucks a terrified gasp out of his lungs, Henry cries out, "No! Jonathan?!"

"Shshshsh, Henry! What's the matter?"

Henry had just let go of Jonathan and retreated a step.

Aaron turns to him, sees his eyes and realizes, "No, no, no, Henry, he's just passed out."

"He's alright?"

"He's okay, Henry. He'll come around."

Henry's color returns. He comes forward, and resumes his hold. "Actually, it's a good thing. I need to do this before he comes to." With one hand on the shoulder, and supporting the forearm with his other hand and rotating it slowly, "There!" Aaron feels it with his hand as ball and socket are married again.

"I think that'll do it. Hand me the bandages quick before he rouses. It'll save him some grief if we wrap him before he wakes." Henry hands Aaron the wide bandages they use on the horses.

They are about done when Jonathan starts to murmur, and stir. His eyes blink themselves back into this world. His voice very hoarse, "That was just practice. Shall we give it another go?" he winces through a grin.

Aaron chuckles. Henry shakes his head. It doesn't take much to convince them that Jonathan is back to his old self.

Henry confesses, "You scared the hell out of me when you fainted! It didn't help that Aaron didn't say anything." Henry is blaming Aaron for his stomach falling to the floor.

Groggy, but still with a little fight left, Jonathan argues, "I didn't faint! It was the sedative, I fell asleep."

"Yeah," Aaron said, chuckling, "You fell asleep very quickly, suddenly in fact. Do you remember anything from before?"

Jonathan thinks back, 'Oh, yeah,' he said to himself in his head. But secretly, he wishes he could erase all the 'Henry Speak' he lavished on Aaron.

Instead, he said in reply, "It's all rather fuzzy," trying to avoid actually lying because he doesn't recall an instance when he ever really lied to Aaron before. Now would be downright unforgivable.

To quickly change the subject Jonathan asks, "Do you think I could have a drink?"

Aaron says to Henry, "Henry, do you mind getting him a drink? I'll just check up on Mr. Selene's status," as he rises to fish out his phone.

"Certainly," Henry obliges, but he winces as he rises from the bale of hay, and Jonathan notices, through his foggy eyes, that Henry has his hand up to support his side as he walks away. Henry returns from his truck with three open bottles. When Aaron's back is turned, Henry helps Jonathan take a swallow.

Soon enough Aaron discovers the boys' antics.
"I meant water, Henry."

"This was closer than the house." He grins. "Besides, it's liquid," Henry reasoned, and takes a swallow. As Aaron approaches, Jonathan quickly takes a couple more big swigs before Aaron motions with his hand, 'Give that to me.'

"Beer and the medication I gave you don't mix, my boy," Aaron admonishes him. Taking the third bottle for himself, he hands Jonathan's bottle to Henry, who was only too glad to be responsible for two.

"Hey, no fair," Jonathan whines as if he is being excluded from a keg party.

"You can't have beer on an empty stomach!" he said, the sedative dampening his cleverness. But not entirely overcoming it.

"Well, once I've had the beer, my stomach won't be empty will it?" Aaron promptly retorts.

Henry chuckles, but winces again. "Good one, cheers!" and he and Aaron tap their bottles together.

Jonathan relentlessly pursues, "You can't have beer when you're working. It's a government policy, and right now you're my doctor." He nods, satisfied.

This time, Henry nods in agreement with Jonathan, and raises his bottle again. "Cheers!" he says, now anticipating that Aaron will give him reason to take another swig. Aaron, having had more years of banter with his buddies than Jonathan and Henry have put together, replies, "Good sir, as your doctor, I declare you well enough for independent care until help arrives and therefore," he paused for another swallow, "I can clock out. Cheers!" he unknowingly obliges Henry. Then Aaron takes a nice long thirst quenching draught just for Jonathan's benefit, and he and Henry start laughing.

Still laughing, Henry remembers a pending assignment and leaves to get Jonathan some water. Henry didn't hide it very well and Jonathan sees it again, Henry wincing.

ONLY WHEN I BREATHE

Jonathan motions to Aaron to come closer, and he whispers, "I think there's something wrong with Henry."

"He's fine, just tired," Aaron reasons.

"No, look again."

Aaron still couldn't tell, so just to humor Jonathan, he turns to Henry and says, "Alright, Henry, point to where it hurts most." Sure enough, Henry points to his back. Aaron palpates and Henry sucks in air as he winces and jumps back from Aaron's touch. It is only when Henry lifts his shirt tail that they see the big bruise, where the horse had kicked Henry in the ribs. Aaron promptly retrieves more bandages as Henry gives Jonathan a sip of water.

"Why didn't you say anything?" Aaron asks as he looks into Henry's face in awe.

Henry says softly so Jonathan can't hear, "You looked busy," his gaze drawn to Jonathan who is getting loopy now from the medication. Aaron refrains from admonishing him any further. But he does give Henry a 'look.'

"It's okay, he would've done the same for me. Besides I'm fine,"

Henry insists.

“You're a credit to your family,” Aaron turns serious. “Your father would be especially proud to have raised a fine young man, son.”

Henry replies as nonchalantly as he could, “Thanks, but, he wasn't alone, you know,” and he veers his eyes from Aaron's gaze, and pretends to be distracted by the bandages that Aaron was winding around his midriff.

Aaron, says as he finishes taping, “That'll do, for the trip anyway. Now we just wait for help. Does it still hurt?” Aaron notices now, the intermittent wincing, and interrupted breathing.

‘Nope, not at all,’ Henry was about to lie through his clenched teeth.

Aaron gives him the 'look' again and shakes his head.

“Well, only when I breathe,” he says instead.

“Breathe through your belly. Okay. Better?”

“Much.” Henry grins as he tries the simple but effective remedy, and says, relieved, “Thanks, Aaron.”

BECAUSE

As Aaron glances at his other charge, Jonathan now enjoying the effects of the sedative, smiles widely through droopy eyelids, "Hey, Aaron, if I tell them I hurt a lot at the hospital, will they give me more of that stuff you gave me when I get there?"

"You do, and I'll have your hide," Aaron warns with a stern tone, trying to hide his amusement at Jonathan's cleverness.

He giggles, and mockingly says in a high-pitched childlike voice, "Yes, Father!" then he giggles some more. Aaron chuckles. His tongue now very much uninhibited, Jonathan advises, "Henry, you really ought to try this shit!" Henry looks toward Aaron like a puppy asking for bacon.

"No." Aaron shakes his head. "Sorry, Henry. You've had too much of that now." And Aaron motions to Henry's bottle.

"Hey wait a minute, which hospital are they taking me?" Jonathan's speech starts to slur. They mention the name. Jonathan's face becomes grim. "I can't go. I won't go."

"Why not?"

"Because."

“What do you mean 'because’?”

“There’s a problem. I can’t go to the hospital like this.”

Jonathan mumbles very softly.

Aaron now understands Jonathan’s dismay. “And you don’t want anyone at the hospital to know,” Aaron clarifies.

“I don’t want anyone to know.”

“Well, I can...” Aaron willingly offers.

“No! No Way.” Jonathan is appalled Aaron would even suggest it.

“How ‘bout Henry?” Aaron suggests, thinking familiarity might help.

“All the more,” Jonathan replies, resolute. He had drawn a line, and there was no getting past it.

“Hmmm, any ideas? I'm sure it's not their first time. You can just swallow a little pride, and let them deal with it at the hospital, just this once.”

“Well, it's *my* first time. And there’s more than just my pride at stake here. My entire dating future, down the tubes.”

“They won’t all find out. Maybe one or at worst, two.”

“And do you realize that by the end of the week, half the girls in town will know,” Jonathan says, shaking his head vigorously, in a drunken kind of way, “and with my luck, it's the half that Henry hasn't dated yet.”

“Stop it, Jonathan. It hurts to laugh.” Henry winces again as he tries to stifle his chuckle.

"How about a male nurse? We can request it."

Jonathan turns his head. "Really! You do realize some are worse with gossip. In our town? It will still *leak* out. I'd rather my shoulder pop out of its socket again." He stands his ground, even with the sedative creeping over his eyes.

"That important, huh?"

All three sit in silence for a while. Then Henry perks up, "I've got an idea." After a bit, Henry comes back with a bucket of liquid and hands it to Aaron who peers in, gets a whiff, then makes a face.

"Are you sure you don't want us to..."

"Absolutely certain. And don't try it while I'm asleep." Jonathan's eyelids close even as he continues to speak, slurring his words. "That's just bad form," he reminds them of some vague male honor code.

So, with great apprehension, Aaron pours a little of the bucket's contents onto Jonathan's crotch.

Henry says, "Oh, no, you have to make it realistic," and promptly douses Jonathan's whole left side with the warm liquid. It is difficult to tell from his silly grin whether Jonathan is truly pleased with the disguise or simply under the effects of his medication.

When Mr. Selene and the other paramedic arrive, Aaron gives them a list of medical information on the boys and he says apologetically, "About Jonathan's ....wet clothes. He sort of got into some unsavory liquid, sorry."

“Not to worry, my friend,” Mr. Selene assures him.

“And thanks for coming right away, Gregory,” Aaron gives him a fond shake.

They promptly wheel Jonathan out to the helicopter, while Henry manages to walk to his ride.

Henry hollers over the din of the helicopter blades, “Aren't you riding with us?”

“I'll be right behind, in my car. I'll need it to get back,” Aaron hollers back and waves.

CHAPTER 7   ARM ON MY SHOULDER

JUST ONCE MORE

Aaron didn't realize that his car wouldn't start until the helicopter had already departed for the hospital. "Damn!" He strikes the steering wheel. Then, in his rearview mirror, he views the barn. After a few moments he takes off for the hospital by the shortest route he knows.

Sometime later, at the hospital, the attending doctor tells Marion and Mrs. Pingrey the boys are both assured good prognoses, but do need to stay a while though. Jonathan is blissfully asleep. But Henry, having thrown generous portions of suave wit around the emergency room, now sits up grinning widely in anticipation, when a young nurse pokes her head in the room, giggles, and winks at him. "Your night nurse is very good looking." Henry rubs his hands in excitement. Momentarily, a handsome *male* nurse walks in and introduces himself, and Henry's face falls.

"You should probably go home and come back later in the day, Marion. They'll be fine." Aaron reassures her.

"Mrs. Pingrey has gone home," she says. "She looked so tired. I told her I would ride home with you. I do hope you don't mind?"

"I think it's perfect. I hope you won't mind," he says leading her to where he parked.

As they exit, she asks, "Aaron, have you had beer? Shall I drive?"

To which he replies, "If you insist," and he waves his hand towards their ride. They both laugh.

The horse is on a fairly good trot when she cautions, "Please, slow down, Aaron."

"It'll take longer," he warns her.

"That's fine, as long as neither of us breaks his neck or worse, both of us. Can you imagine what people will think if they found us on the ground dead in the morning?"

"Well, if we still have smiles on our faces, they will think good thoughts for us." They laugh again. It is beautiful country in the moonlight, the stars singing their serenade with a clear voice. A little further and Marion gets drowsy and nods in his arms.

"Marion, Marion, stay awake just a little longer. It's important. There's something I have to show you."

He covers her eyes with his hand and leads the horse with the other. Finally, the trees part to reveal a lake. He winds the lead onto the saddle horn. The wind had died down earlier. Now it is so calm and still that you can see the reflection of the stars twinkling. Without touching her arm he reaches into a side pocket, makes a fist and stretches his arm out in front of him towards the lake.

"Alright. Guess."

She feels his outstretched arm. "You're pointing at something."

"Maybe, go on."

"The air is different here, cooler, but no breeze, and there are insects, and, frogs. It's a lake! You're pointing at a lake, and the night is clear, so the stars are shining on the lake. I want to see." And she pulls his hand from her eyes at the same time he turns his fist slowly, and opens the palm of his hand to reveal the twinkling of the ring, offset by the stars on the lake's glassy surface.

"Oh Aaron!" She picks up the ring with both hands.

"Will you marry me?"

"How could this be, tonight?"

"Marion, will you marry me?" he repeats.

"How did you know? Tonight?"

"Shall I ask one more time?"

She smiles into his face. "Just once more."

"Marion, will you..."

She interrupts him with a kiss.

FOR BEING HERE

Head still resting on the white pillow, Jonathan opens his tired eyes and puts his hand to his shoulder. He can feel pain's fingers groping, trying to get a hold. Then he turns his head a little and he notices Mrs. Pingrey reading a book while exercising on her portable stair climber machine. 'Hmmm,' he thinks to himself, 'Mother thought she was going home last night. She never left!' Mrs. Pingrey, ever vigilant, notices he has awakened and comes near.

"Of course," she says, "after that ordeal you have earned a kiss on the forehead," as she plants one on him.

"Mrs. P., I haven't brushed my teeth," he cringes.

"You'll have to do worse than that to keep me away," she grins.

"You never went home!" he said, realizing, "You've been here all night."

"How can you tell? I brushed *my* teeth! I even brought a change of clothes!"

He grins. "I only suspected, and you just confirmed it."

She laughs out loud. "Clever boy!"

He tries to chuckle but he aches, so instead he says, "I learn from the best." He looks at her lovingly through tired eyes. Then he realizes, "Mrs. P., where's Henry?"

"Next door, giving the ladies an overdose of charm. Want me to fetch him?" Her smile tells him that Henry is fine.

"Wait, not just yet." He gathers his thoughts and his courage to reveal to her his heart wounds.

"When I was laying there in the barn, alone, I thought I saw Moriah. But Aaron told me later, she was there to be with me, not there to take me away. For a moment, I wished she could stay. But I didn't wish to leave with her. I didn't wish to die, even though it hurt enough to want to die. Mrs. Pingrey," he whispers to her now, "I wasn't very brave," as he raises his chin so he could look her in the eye.

"On the contrary, dearest, on the contrary." She doles out a comforting smile.

He smiles back, then shuts his eyes, turns his head away slightly and takes a long deep breath.

She feels a squeeze in her heart, "Are you hurting, dear?"

He opens his eyes and turns to her. "Yes, Mrs. P., but not the same as before."

Mrs. Pingrey, instead of hugging him, thought, 'she'd better save it for later when it won't cause him distress,' and squeezes his hand.

Then Jonathan looks up bright eyed. “I never thanked you for being there when,” he pauses to correct himself, “for *being here* for me, as I go through this. Thank you.

“Well, we're just a couple of uncivilized ingrates! I never thanked you for being there,” she pauses to correct herself, “for being here *for me,* as I go through this. Thank you.”

This reminds Jonathan about the little girl in her poem, and he says with urgency, “I have to tell you something important. I know about the little girl. That night, you were in the bathroom.”

“Yes, It's alright. I know you know. I knew that night.”
Jonathan wonders how she could possibly know.

That night in her kitchen, Mrs. Pingrey took a mental note as she returned from the bathroom. Her observation skills honed over the years, she notices, the program isn't how she left it on the counter before she stepped away.

“I'm sorry, I didn't mean to pry. It's just you were so upset, I had to find a way to help you. Then when you returned, I didn't know what to say.”

“Don't apologize. You saying nothing is exactly what I needed from you at the time. Besides, if I didn't want you to know, I would have taken the program to the bathroom with me.”

They both laugh. And when their laughter subsides, they stay deep in thought for a while until suddenly Jonathan has a tremendous urgent need for a pen. Mrs. Pingrey, familiar with the feeling and his state of mind, quickly whips out a pen from her bag. He scribbles and scribbles, then looks up at her.

"I'll need to edit, but basically I think I've got most of it from my head onto paper. Do you want to see?" He offers it to her.

"Is it better now, or later, when you've finished?"

"Now is better. It's important." Just then they hear voices from just outside the door. She opens her hand, and he folds it and gives it to her for safe keeping in her pocket.

Henry enters Jonathan's room. "Mrs. Pingrey! I thought I saw you sitting in my room last night but I was too out of it. Couldn't tell if it was a dream or real. And I couldn't talk." He gives her a long hug. She reminds herself not to squeeze too tightly.

"You've been here all night! You're the best!"

"How do you boys do that?"

"Do what? What'd I do?"

"I brushed my teeth. I've changed my clothes! Do I smell funny?" She raises her arms to smell.

The boys reply simultaneously, "You always smell lovely!" They look at each other and grin.

"Then how do you know I haven't gone home?"

Henry's eyes dart back and forth between Jonathan and Mrs. Pingrey. "I only suspected," he says apologetically.

Then Mrs. Pingrey chimes in "And I just confirmed it for you!" They all laugh.

Suddenly, Henry becomes somber. He takes her by the shoulders and plants a kiss on her cheek, and hugs her.

"Ooh! I don't get that often enough from you. Why so mushy, Henry?"

He kisses her again on the other cheek. "The first one's for being here for us, and the second one's for being 'Our Mrs. Pingrey.'"

The boys are all smiles.

As Mrs. Pingrey steps out to get a bite to eat, Jonathan's phone rings. It's Aaron. He had tried Henry's but Henry didn't hear it ringing in the other room. Aaron had something important to tell the boys.

After talking to Aaron, Jonathan tells Henry as he dials, "If Aaron feels this way, just think how she feels. I'm calling her!"

"Oh, are you *ever* going to need a change of address!" Henry warns, amused.

"What? What's she going to do to me? I'm in a hospital, safest place on earth! Heh, heh, heh..." Jonathan places a call to Marion, and Henry sits by his side grinning and listening intently.

QUICKSAND

It has only been a few minutes since Jonathan and Henry were on a call with Aaron.

Jonathan, grinning deviously into the phone, asks, "Where were you all night? Why didn't you call?"
"Uh, we took it slow coming home," Marion answers apprehensively.
"I'd say. Aaron brought you home then?"

She watches Aaron now pouring out tea from the kettle. He is wearing Jonathan's bathrobe. It says 'GLADIATOR' across the back and Swim team Captain below it. She gathers her robe tighter around her neck.

"Yes!" She was glad she could answer truthfully.
"and dropped you off?" Jonathan continues, "It sure took a while, ride problems?"
"Yes, yes, definitely ride problems." She bites a nail.
"So what happened?"
"What do you mean?" She furrows her eyebrows, anticipating a question she can't answer comfortably.
"What happened to the car?"
"Oh, the car, Aaron had to leave the car, yes, and we got home by

horse," she says hoping the interrogation would stop.

Meanwhile, Henry is pressing his face onto a clear plastic clipboard. Jonathan couldn't keep from laughing but it sent shooting pain through his shoulder. He groans, still smiling.

"Jonathan, are you alright?"
"Yes, Mother, it's just Henry. He's making me laugh because he knows it'll hurt." He throws the tissue box. A corner of the box hits Henry on the head.
"Owww!"

A surly nurse pokes her head in, shakes it, and retreats. And the boys start laughing with as little noise as possible. But Marion hears him snickering, "Well, you're laughing so you must be feeling better."
"Yes, yes, don't worry. So what are you doing now?"
"Really, Jonathan! I just washed my hair just now."
"Why?"
"Now, does a mother have to give her son a reason for washing her hair?"

"Where's the horse?"
"Good grief, Jonathan!" and she promptly hangs up on him.
"Ohhh!" she surrenders and sits.
Aaron, who has turned to face her now, of course, is thoroughly entertained because she is flustered.
"I don't do this very well do I?" she asks, wrapping the robe closer around her neck, as she stands to leave.

Aaron turns back to making tea.

"I'm going upstairs. I really need to get out of this bathrobe right away. I mean, I need to get dressed. I feel naked in this thing. I mean… Oh gosh, Aaron?"

"Yes?" he says over his shoulder.

"Have you ever been in quicksand?" She drops the question on the floor as she darts upstairs to change into more safe clothes.

"In fact, in South Amer..." he stops abruptly as he turns and sees he is talking all by himself.

ON MY HONOR

But, before Jonathan dialed Marion, Aaron had secretly called Jonathan and Henry earlier.

Standing in the guest bathroom downstairs, Aaron looks up to the ceiling. He hears Marion turn the shower on upstairs. He turns sideways to the mirror to see the bold letters across the back of the bathrobe, 'GLADIATOR' and beneath it 'Swim team Captain.' He's not sure how he's going to break it to the boys that he had to sequester Jonathan's bathrobe due to an unforeseen need. After all, he swore an oath to Marion!

“Why are you telling me this?” Jonathan's voice grew serious so Henry naturally gravitates to him and signals Jonathan to put the phone on speaker.

“For one thing, this is a small town. People saw us leave the hospital together last night, and for another,” Aaron sighs, “My horse is parked in your yard.”

Jonathan and Henry almost burst out laughing. Jonathan pushes the mute button and they both let loose their laughter, then regain composure quickly, so Jonathan can turn off the mute. Henry hand signals Jonathan to make Aaron explain, and to lengthen the conversation.

“You mean you can tell me stuff *I didn't ask* to know, but you can't tell me stuff *I'm asking* to know?”

“She made me promise, 'not ‘til the time is right,' she said.” Aaron doesn't realize he is now pacing inside the tiny bathroom.

“And so you're calling me to tell me nothing has happened?” Jonathan was speaking slowly, choosing each word.

“I wouldn't be calling you if something did, would I?” Aaron grimaces, “So sorry, I didn't mean that the way it sounded.”

Henry couldn't help but jump in, “I'm having doubts about your decency. No decent man would call to say nothing happened!”

“Thanks for listening in, Henry. I don't have time to explain this a second time.” He looks upwards.

“Well, what the HECK is the problem then?”

Aaron rubs his forehead. “Well, I did have to borrow Jonathan's bathrobe.” Aaron winces, bracing himself for Jonathan's reaction. Henry nods. Now he understands.

Jonathan is aghast. “My bathrobe? Are you standing there NAKED in MY bathrobe?!”

“Not entirely. I borrowed underwear.”

“What? Whose?” Jonathan was trying with great difficulty, not to visualize the doctor in his underwear.

“Your mother's! Well, of course, THEY'RE YOURS!!” Now, exasperated, Aaron regrets calling. He thinks he might have been better off with the townspeople's rumors.

"Doctor, you're in MY house, in MY underwear, in My bathrobe, and you call Me to tell me 'NOTHING'S HAPPENED'?!"

"On my honor, nothing happened!" Aaron looks ruefully into the phone.

"Well, how can we rely on your honor, if that's what's in question?" Henry offers a dilemma. Again, the boys are joyfully guffawing on their end, while the phone is on mute.

Aaron takes a deep breath, as if he is trying to start from the beginning, "Boys, you know I've always been upfront with you. Alright, then, I swear on my mother's soul."

"Nothing happened?" Henry reiterates.

"Nothing happened." Aaron looks up. He hears Marion's shower turn off upstairs.

And Jonathan being thorough, just as good as makes him promise, "Nor *will* happen?"

"Nor will." Aaron breathes a sigh of relief when they all finally hang up.

But at the hospital, Jonathan and Henry giggle like a couple of teenage girls with disturbingly deep voices.

Still trying to catch his breath, Jonathan says, "I can't believe he fell for that," and they go through another wave of laughter.

Aaron couldn't explain that, after he had proposed, and as they turned away from the lake, an animal spooked the horse and it reared. He and Marion had fallen into the lake, spent part of the night by a fire where they warmed up and dried off a little, and eventually headed home. Their clothes still damp and muddy, needed a good wash and were now spinning in the dryer. Aaron in the meantime, had to borrow Jonathan's robe because nothing else would fit around his middle. Meanwhile, Marion and he were having tea and cakes while they waited for their laundry.

MY BEST FRIEND

Now dry and warm, Marion and Aaron settle into chairs and continue to reminisce.

“I'm glad I came back when I did. It was good to see you and Edmund very happy. Edmund was a good man.” And then he chuckles, “I wouldn't have guessed what it would feel like to return after so many years. I never before that day knew such joy.” He and Marion laugh together at the memory they share.

Aaron recalls, many years ago, in front of Edmund's house, when a little boy came running up and said, “Hello, I'm Jonathan. Father says you are his best friend in the whole world.”

“Oh, he did, did he?” Aaron sits on his heels then extends his hand to shake but Jonathan throws him a hug and topples him backwards. Then as Aaron helps Jonathan to his feet, he looks up to a pair of cheerful faces, Edmund's and Marion's.

Edmund puts his arm over Aaron's shoulder and leads him to the house. “It's been too long, my friend.”

“I see five years hasn't touched you above the waist,” Aaron says to Ed.

"Marion takes good care of me," he says, resting his hand on his happy belly.

"Marion," Aaron peers in Marion's direction, "your waist is the same. Does that mean Ed takes less care of you than you do him?"

They all laugh.

Then, at the front porch, Jonathan proudly presents to Aaron, a much bigger, brown haired little boy. "This, here, is my best friend Henry. Like you and father, I will watch over him and protect him and love all he loves as I would my own. And he would do the same for me."

"Well, you are both fortunate to have such a staunch friend in each other," Aaron says as he ruffles Jonathan's dark wavy hair. "Good to meet you Henry," Aaron greets him pleasantly.

Henry promptly extends his hand to shake.

Now, as Aaron's and Marion's laughter subside, a seriousness falls over Aaron's voice. "It feels like only yesterday. And at the same time, so long ago. So much has happened. You know Marion, *I couldn't love these two any greater if they were my own."*

And with those words still fresh on his lips, Marion felt she could finally open the door that she had for too many years feared.

THE WORLD ANEW

Marion says, "Now, there's something I have been meaning to tell you." At first she seems uneasy, but then decides to just plunge into it. "The boys, they are not Edmund's biological sons."

Aaron in grips of disbelief, "Impossible, Edmund loved you. How could you have? You couldn't have. I just don't see it in you. But her face belied that she was telling the truth. The boys weren't Edmund's.

Aghast, he blurts out, "How could you do that to Edmund? Marion!" His face, downcast at the thought that the woman he had held in such high esteem all his life, would betray his best friend, no, THEIR best friend. It was as if he himself were betrayed.

"Calm down, Aaron, and think for a moment. Edmund knew. He knew everything all along."

Many years ago Edmund said to Marion, "Let me be the father the child needs. No matter what happens, I promise to love the child as my own."

Marion continued with her story, "And Ed was true to his word. You could see it in his eyes, when Henry was born and Edmund first held him in his arms. Eventually Jonathan came, and Ed first set his eyes on him. He said through tears of unbounded joy, 'I shall love them so much that even I couldn't tell the difference.'"

Aaron understood, "Ed would do that out of love for you. I knew it even then. He really loved you."
She looked into Aaron's face and said, "And he loved you."
Slowly, Aaron began to realize the weight of her words.
"Henry and Jonathan, they're mine?" she nods, unsure of his reaction. "I have sons? Marion, I HAVE TWO SONS!"
"Yes!" Now she knows she can smile.

Aaron tells Marion that from the first time he met the boys, "I had always felt something special, something between us. Marion, I have to see them, please, I know we were just there, but I must see them."

When they arrive at the hospital, the nurse explains that the boys were heavily medicated for their pain and are probably too groggy to know they have visitors, but Aaron and Marion can give it a try.

Aaron enters first and comes around to the top of the bed. He wants to hug his son but Jonathan is asleep. He couldn't love them both any more than he already did, and has all these years. They were the same boys as they were hours ago, but today, this very moment, Aaron's heart was seeing their faces with new eyes. He ruffled his son's hair and kissed him on the head. And this made Jonathan stir. Although foggy from his medicine, Jonathan recognized Marion at the foot of the bed but realized Aaron, being closer, may have just kissed him.

“Did you just... Never mind, I think it's the medication talking.” Then he drifted off again.

Aaron didn't know whether to laugh or cry so he did both. He looked at Marion with tearful happy eyes.
“My son! He's my son, Marion.”
“Mother?” Jonathan pries his eyelids open. “Is one of us dying?
“No, dear, no one is dying.”
“Then why is he crying?” His eyes flutter in Aaron's direction but he couldn't focus, and he closes his eyes again.
Aaron looks towards Marion as if to say, “Can I tell him?! I can't wait!”
She nods, “Of course.”
“Jonathan, can you hear me? I’ve always loved you as my own. Only now, I can actually say it, you’re my son! Jonathan, did you hear me?”

Jonathan is breathing very softly, and slowly. He has fallen asleep. Marion shook her head. “We'll have to wait. Let's go see Henry.” Marion pulls Aaron by the arm towards the door. But Aaron couldn't take his eyes off his new son. He smiles, then just before he turns towards the door,

Jonathan stirs, “Aaron, Henry doesn't do mushy.” His eyes are still closed, and it is almost a whisper, but Aaron hears him.

Aaron is chuckling as he gazes into Henry's face. “Marion, I never realized it before, Jonathan, he looks like a younger me! Henry, not so much like me, more like, my father! Ha!” Aaron couldn't believe he hadn't seen it before.

He couldn't explain logically, now that he knew about his sons, although not much else has changed, he was seeing them and the whole world anew.

"Henry," he whispers close to Henry's ear, *"You're my son."* Aaron seemed pleased to hear the words come from his lips. And with that, he kissed Henry on the head, and lost a tear. Henry stirs and murmurs something unintelligible, but his eyes remain closed. Aaron and Marion decide to step outside to let Henry sleep.

APOLOGY ACCEPTED

After being released from the hospital, and too excited to wait any longer, Jonathan and Henry pile the last of Jonathan's belongings into Henry's truck. Marion hands a basket brimming with a hefty picnic lunch to Henry which he passes to Jonathan to hold while he drives.

"Jonathan, call me if you need anything," she reminds him for the fourteenth time that day.

Henry starts to chuckle so she tousles his hair. Jonathan shoves him by the shoulder. "Stop, Henry. I Love you, Mum."

"I Love you, too." Then she turns to Henry. "I Love you, too, dear," as she pokes her head in through the window to give him a kiss. They pull away in the fully loaded pickup and wave.

"It's going to be quieter around here," says Mrs. Pingrey as she sighs.

"Oh, I don't know, but it's a step in the right direction."

"Indeed," says Aaron, who steps out of the house just in time to wave.

They watch the pickup go down the street. The boys are grinning, enjoying their newfound freedom already. The truck turns a corner and slides into a driveway, all of seven houses away, where they proceed to unload Jonathan's belongings onto the porch of Henry's place.

"Hold up. There's something I need to say."
"What?" Jonathan continues unloading.
"I never really said it before."
Jonathan turns to face him.
"I never said, 'I'm sorry,'"
"What about?"
"About, you know, anything I could have done differently."
"Well, that's kind of vague."
"Just the same, I'm really sorry. Just that, I never meant to..."

Jonathan suddenly strikes him in the face then immediately cradles his painful knuckles while Henry cries out,
"Awwww!" and nurses his lip. "What the...I'm bleeding! What did you do that for?"
"You told me to hit you."
"I did not!"
"I thought this had to do with the other night."
"What other night?"
"The other night when you told me to hit you."
"Well, yeah. But, that really hurt!"
"Well, that is the point, isn't it? Apology," he grunts from the pain in his hand, "accepted!" Jonathan takes a deep breath, and releases it with measure.

"Do we feel better now?" Jonathan says, in an irritated voice. Henry moves his jaw left to right, winces, then realization comes to him. "Well, actually, yeah, I do."

“Alright then,” Jonathan says, hiding a grin, “is there anything *else* you need to tell me?”
“No,” Henry replies as he sucks his swelling lip.
“Right. Let’s get on with it then,” Jonathan goads Henry into turning back to the heap in the truck beckoning to be tossed into Henry's place.

ABOUT MY MOTHER

About an hour later, scuffling noise emanates from the living room, and Henry hollers, "I'll tell mum you said that!" Jonathan dodges multiple flying objects.
"Married or not...they just had really good..." Jonathan adds with an impish grin.
"Don't you LIE like that about my mother! She wasn't like that! Take it back or I'll...."
SMASH! Then the sound of a body falling to the floor.
"JONATHAN!" Henry's voice, laced with fear, "You were supposed to duck!" Slap, slap, slap. "Jonathan? Jonathan, wake up!"
Jonathan sits up with his hand to his head. His eyes slowly come back into focus. "Rapport, they had really good rapport. What did you hit me with? Owwww!"
"Damn, you're bleeding!"
"You made me bleed on my favorite shirt!" Jonathan whines.
"Calm down. You can wash it." Henry helps him onto a chair.
"I never wash this shirt. This is a souvenir. Awwww!"
"Here, press this towel on your cut. It's deeper than I first thought. SHIT! We'll have to ask Aaron to fix that up. Come on, give me your phone."
"Use yours."

"I can't. I forgot to charge it." Henry grabs Jonathan's phone. "Aarrgh! This one's out of juice, too." He grabs the keys to the truck. "Come on, I'll take you over. I bet he's still there. Are you woozy?"
"No!"
Henry takes Jonathan's elbow and ushers him to the truck.
"I can get to the truck by myself. Stop pushing!" Jonathan whines and stubbornly resists.

Henry slams the truck door. The truck won't start so they make for Marion's house on foot. Quick footsteps and panting sounds alert Mrs. Pingrey who is in the room above. She hurries down the hall towards the stairs just as the screen door slams behind them.

Aaron is nowhere in sight so Henry calls out, "Mother? Aaron? Mother, is Aaron still here?"
Mrs. Pingrey appears and pulls up a chair, "Oh, my word! Sit down, dear. I'll get Aaron."
Marion rushes in from the garden and asks, "What happened?"
Henry nudges Jonathan and under his breath says, "Shut up."
But to Marion he says, "We were putting up a shelf, and he fell off a ladder."

"Jonathan, you just got out of the hospital. Can't you last a week?" Marion looks under the towel. "Ooooh!"

Aaron comes in. "How bad?"
"Oh, maybe two, or three," Marion guesses.
Then Aaron asks, "How'd it happen?" as he opens his bag.

Henry's about ready to recount his story, but he and Jonathan both know they have difficulty lying to Aaron. And Jonathan looks up, bright-eyed and smiling. He can't help but enjoy seeing Henry squirm in his self-imposed deathbed.

"He started it! It's his fault. He said...he said..." and he couldn't repeat it exactly as Jonathan said it. It's embarrassing. His mother is right there! And Aaron, too. Henry turns to Jonathan who is now beyond snickering and is in stitches but has a hand to the strawberry printed kitchen towel on his head. Henry, trying to preserve his integrity, turns toward his mother.

"He was mouthing off."
"And that was a good enough reason to hit your brother in the head and make him bleed?" Marion says, half smiling, waiting for an acceptable explanation.
"He said reprehensible things!" Henry desperately wants to express the gravity of Jonathan's crime.

"I didn't actually say it. I can't help it if you thought it!" Jonathan offers in his defense, still smiling.

Henry throws him a warning glance. Jonathan thought it wise to hold his tongue and put on a serious face. Aaron chuckles to himself, glances over at Henry, and then notices his lower lip.

Henry continues in his defense, "And besides, I didn't hit him. I threw something towards him, and he failed to duck."

Marion's left eyebrow rises, a question mark drawn on her forehead. "Henry Lorenzo," she pauses to let it sink in. The rest she said with her eyes, 'I need better than that!'

Finally, as a last attempt to defend his good name, Henry says, "I was defending a lady's honor!" There, he's satisfied. That's a good one. He doesn't have to give details, but he's off the hook.

"Well, in that case, you can hit him again!" Marion proclaims with the sharpness of a gavel.

"See!" Henry hits Jonathan on the arm.
"Hey, don't strike a man when he's down." Jonathan cowers, still smiling.

"Keep still, Jonathan! I could hurt you!" Aaron warns him.
"Huh? Whatever happened to 'I'd shoot myself before I'd hurt any one of you'?"
"That was before."
"Before what?" both boys pipe in.

Aaron and Marion briefly exchange glances, but the boys were too sharp to miss it.
"Before your mother and I had a talk."

Marion smiles at Aaron and says, "I guess it's time?" He smiles back, and resumes patching Jonathan up. Then she rises, reaches into a drawer and brings out an envelope. "I guess I should start from the beginning." She pulls out a picture of a baby girl. "Her name was Thallia Marion, like your grandmother. I had her at a very young age, and we lost her when she was little, before you two were born." She pauses, "There's more."

DOWN SUPERBLY

"Your father loved you both no differently than if you were his very own. And Aaron has loved you as though you were his very own even though he knew that you were Edmund's sons."
"Oh, and there's one more thing," Marion says, her voice, now serious. "He's a bit of a thief!"

The boys glance at Aaron, wide-eyed. Aaron says quickly, "Don't look at me, your mother is the clever one."
"He's stolen my heart! We're getting married!" She promptly kisses him.
The boys chime, "'Bout time!" They all laugh happily.
The boys get up to congratulate them with a hug.
"You are happy? About Aaron, I mean?" Marion now standing close with a hand to Aaron's heart.
"Ecstatic!" said one. "Couldn't be happier!" said the other, but their reaction seemed somehow, lacking, Marion thought. She threw a reluctant glance to Aaron.
Aaron spoke for her, "I think your mother expected you both to be a little more surprised."

Henry and Jonathan look at each other. They had to spill it. Henry went first. "Thallia's marker, I discovered it by accident a while back. Then I took Jonathan there."

"We've never known you to be anything but faithful to father. But, the marker told us enough to know our arrival spilled over into your life with him. So we didn't ask any questions." Jonathan took delight in admitting how they felt about their mother. Marion couldn't be more proud of her sons than this moment.

Henry explains further, "Jonathan told me about parts of his dream at the hospital. I had one too, kind of foggy, of you talking," he averted his eyes towards Aaron, "and crying, and other mushy stuff. I was a little weirded out. So I didn't tell Jonathan my dream."

Jonathan suddenly pieces it together, "Then it wasn't a dream? At the hospital, That's why you were crying! You had just been told! I remember thinking one of us was dying!"

"Well, I hadn't imagined your reaction to be like this, but I am pleased at how you both are taking it." He couldn't help but get sentimental. "I'm sorry I scared you," Aaron laughs through his teary eyes.

Henry gets serious and takes on an admonishing tone, "You scared *him* into thinking he was dying, you scared *me* into thinking you're a strange man who kisses patients on their heads as they sleep, and you *steal* from our mother! Yeah, You've got this father and husband thing down *superbly*, Aaron!"

Aaron was laughing so hard, he had to wipe tears. Their unbridled laughter assured him of their acceptance.

Mrs. Pingrey walks in, "Oh, that Sadie, she got out again. Had to chase her down the street! What'd I miss?"

CHICKEN BONE

The next day, as Marion and Mrs. Pingrey ready some finger foods, Mrs. Pingrey mildly protests, "I can understand sending the other two, but Jonathan too? Right out of the hospital?"

"Oh, Mrs. Pingrey, he'll be fine. Just a little wet. Besides, he's actually the mastermind. The other two were only accomplices. They all deserve to be out in the mud and rain. Imagine, having a laugh at the cost of my nerves!"

Aaron is out in the pouring rain with the boys at the lake, as near as he can remember to where he and Marion fell in the mud that night he proposed. They are sifting through the dirt and mud, basically dredging for the ring. Aaron explains to the boys, when Marion realized it was missing yesterday, she fell to fits of crying and hadn't stopped since. She was still crying when he left her at the house today. They must find it. A replacement was out of the question. Marion said to him that it has a little nick that she thought was absolutely adorable, and that she could tell the ring apart from any other. Besides, Aaron said, "That ring is like my appendage. I've carried it around for ages waiting for the right time. It's like a part of me. It's as important to me as it is to her."

Meanwhile, at the house, cars are filling Marion's driveway, and the house is full of music and laughter. Marion put out her nice china and wine. She and Mrs. Pingrey are dry and cozy and are enjoying teacakes with guests.

On the other hand, out at the lake, Aaron and the boys, all wet where they aren't covered in mud, having worked through lunch, are now tired and hungry. But they aren't about to give up. This is a really big deal! They can't very well let Marion down. And not one of them wants to be the one to suggest giving up. They are so focused that they don't realize a lightning storm has rolled in, and they are quite vulnerable to the elements. They are staunch men, no doubt, but not even the bravest of men would try to defy the lightning gods. One good bolt near the sopping threesome is enough to send them flying for cover. They have good sense to duck into the truck where they collect themselves, and Henry pipes in, "Alright, I'm not suggesting we give up. Not one of us decided to leave, but that last bolt was definitely a sign that we should go home and try this another day!" One of them seconded the motion, "Agreed," so, Aaron started the engine of his truck.

As they near the house, they see the cars, and through the window, the people, and closer still, hear the music. They trudge into the mudroom and are greeted by Marion. By the looks on their dejected faces, she should have surmised that they are empty-handed, but she looks surprisingly happy.

She has this look of great affection, and tenderness that it is uncanny. "I am so touched and proud of all of you, especially you," and she pinches Jonathan's cheek a little too hard that he scowls.

You three are truly the noblest, bravest, finest gentlemen to step forward to help a lady at her darkest hour. She hugs the boys. To the embarrassment of the boys who are within hearing distance, she gives an especially big kiss to Aaron. Henry and Jonathan, feeling strangely awkward, tried to look away, but they couldn't help but look back directly at Aaron and stare as he made sounds and motions as if he was choking on a piece of chicken bone. Aaron pulls away from Marion's lips brusquely. The boys' jaws begin to hang down while Aaron, purses his adequate lips, and reveals a shiny gold object between his teeth. This he promptly pulls out with his muddy fingers to further reveal a twinkling diamond .

Aaron exclaims in utter bewilderment, "Marion!" to which Marion replies, "Oh, Aaron, you've found it!" And she snatches it from him, and slips it on her finger for safe keeping. All three muddy gentlemen are speechless.

Henry finds his voice first.
"You found it! Why didn't you call us?"

Marion goes to the sink and fetches them warm wet towels to clean up. She is smiling but not talking. Aaron starts guffawing, and Jonathan could have kicked himself right then when he realized,

"You had it all the time!"

Marion hands him his towel, "Here Mr. Mastermind! That teaches you to play tricks on your mother over the phone!"
To Aaron who is still chuckling, she hands a towel and lovingly

accuses, "Mr. Accomplice!"

Then she turns to Henry. But he tries to deny culpability and whines, "But I didn't *do* anything!"
"Precisely, 'Mr. Guilty by Omission,'" Marion says, as she hands him his towel.

Mrs. Pingrey pokes her head in the doorway, and says mockingly, "By the looks on your three faces, I surmise that the ring has been recovered?"

Then another friend of the family appears from behind Mrs. Pingrey's shoulder and comments, "What fine luck! Imagine finding that tiny ring in this torrent!" He can't stop laughing, and has to leave the room. Moments later, laughter emanates from the living room.

Eventually Aaron and his sons get cleaned up enough to join the guests, but not enough to hide all the evidence of where they had been. The three men's embarrassment of being the object of Marion's retaliation, easily give way to laughter as they are in the company of their closest friends anyway. The guests are all in good spirits and only too glad to receive the happy news and join them in celebrating as Marion and Aaron officially announce their engagement.

HERE TAKE THIS

That evening, after the engagement party, Henry and Jonathan return to their new home. Jonathan picks up some tips on Henry's cure all.

"Do you have any glass cleaner?" he asks Henry.
"Just use some beer. There's an open bottle on the table."

A little later, he asks, "I got a cut, do you have any antibacterial ointment?"
Henry hands him a bottle of beer, " A little of this will do."

Later still, when all was quiet, all of a sudden Jonathan runs up the hall with a hand over his face, "I got something in my eye! Henry!" Panicking now from the pain, he hollers, "Henry, where are you?"

"I'm in here!" Henry hollers from the bathroom. Fortunately, the door is open. Jonathan appears at the open doorway. Henry is standing in the bathroom rummaging through a drawer with one hand, and holding a bottle of beer in the other.

"I've got something in my eye! Hurry! Awww, It hurts! Do something!"

"I heard you, here, take this," Henry says, as he hands Jonathan the bottle. And as Henry turns back to continue rummaging for eye drops, Jonathan takes the beer and sloshes a goodly amount in his ailing eye. "ARRRRGH!"

"What the hell did you just do?" Henry screams, as he shoves Jonathan's face under the faucet and turns on a gentle stream of water.
"You said to use the beer!" Jonathan's voice bounces off the sink.

"No, I didn't!"
"Yes, you did!"

"No, I didn't!"
"Yes, you did! You handed me the bottle and said, and I quote, 'HERE, TAKE THIS!'"

With Henry pacing in the background, Marion stands in her kitchen, Jonathan sitting before her. She puts Aaron on speaker phone, and with one hand on Jonathan's head, she tells Aaron,

"Well, Henry rinsed it for about twenty minutes," she says, unsure. "Jonathan says he can see fine." Marion with her hand still over Jonathan's head, now lifts his eyelid with her thumb and bends closer for better inspection. "But, I asked the boys if…"

"What, Marion?"

"Well, I suppose I shouldn't worry, but, you know that foamy stuff you see on slugs?"

BEER vs. SECRETS

"Henry, can you drive him over so I can take a look? Then you boys can stay and watch the game with me if you like," Aaron suggests.

Later, over at the ranch Henry carries beer and food to the den and finds the game on the television. Meanwhile, in the kitchen, Aaron speaks to Jonathan softly, "Do you want to find out tonight?"

Jonathan shrugs, "Good a night as any. We've got an excuse to have beer." They both grin and glance at Henry who is turned away facing the television screen. They watch the game, they drink, and laugh, and drink some more. The game is almost over. It seems Henry can drink a lot of beer. Aaron and Jonathan talk again in the kitchen, reassessing their strategy.

"We're not going to kill him with all this beer are we? He's had a lot!"

Aaron says, "Nah! He's had a lot of pretzels. He'll be fine." Aaron already appears drunk so Jonathan has misgivings about the reliability of Aaron's statement.

"Just the same, let's stop after the next one and give it up. I don't want anything to happen to him." They pick up some more beer and nuts and head back into the other room. "Mother would kill me if something did."

They test Henry with a trial question. Henry obliges them with an answer they know he would not otherwise divulge unless he was drunk. Then they all laugh loudly. That's it. His tongue is loose!

So Jonathan gives it a shot. "Hey, Henry, 'member the night we flew in the helicopter? How the heck did you get the horse to, you know,... on command?"

As drunk as he is, Henry is able to tell them several versions, each of which is good for a laugh. They all know he is being funny.

Aaron presses him for the real answer. "No, come on, really. How?"

Henry confesses, "I cheated. I found a puddle, sopped it up with a rag and wrung the rag over the bucket. Easy!"

They all laugh heartily.

Soon after, it gets quiet. It seems they all have had their fill, and nod off where they sat. Jonathan is in an especially weird position over the arm rest of an armchair, as if he was reaching across it for something and fell asleep in mid-action.

Henry opens one eye to check his adversaries and sees Aaron, very much the image of a hibernating bear. Then, he notices Jonathan's substantial drooling. "Out cold!" Henry snickers with satisfaction. He tilts the plant in a brass pot nearby, sloshing the beer. If the ficus were human, it would be teetering. Henry gets up, quite sober, and rather pompously, he says to himself, "And *that's* how you protect national secrets! Feed the enemy "False, albeit plausible information!"

Aaron then grunts and rolls over to stand up. Henry isn't surprised that he is sober as well. They both start laughing. Aaron puts an arm over Henry's shoulder as they walk over to the adjoining kitchen.

"Do you think you'll ever tell him what it really was?"

Henry says, "Nah, not even under pain of death. I mean, how do you tell your twin brother that you couldn't get the damn horse to cooperate so you had no other recourse but to fill the bucket yourself."

Henry chuckles at the memory of himself, in the back of the barn standing before a bucket with one hand to the wall. Henry's snickering is dying down, while Aaron's laughter is getting louder.

"Har, har, har...Jonathan will never forgive me." Still laughing, Aaron pauses to catch his breath, "I thought I smelled beer in the bucket that day!" Suddenly, Henry's belly spilled over with a deluge of laughter, joining Aaron's, clearly revealing their undeniable lack of remorse.

Meanwhile, in the other room, within earshot, Jonathan slurps up most of his drool, and opens his unexpectedly lucid eyes, then pushes his face up from the remaining puddle on the leather armrest.

"And *that* my friend, is how you get National Secrets from the ENEMY!!"

CHAPTER 8   SEEKING AND FULFILLING

ASKING FOR FORGIVENESS

The following afternoon, Jonathan confirms the address on the slip of paper his mother gave him earlier, then tucks it in his pocket. He knocks on the door, and fidgets with the hat in his hands as he waits. The door opens. 'This must be Mrs. Lambert,' he thought.

“Hello,” says Jonathan with a smile.

“Well, hello,” she replies, as she wipes her hands on a dishtowel.

As Jonathan begins to say, “I'm...”

“Jonathan!” she exclaims when she realizes who it is. It surprises her to know it is him because they had never met before. “You're just the way my husband described. Come in, please. I'll take you to him.”

“That's very kind of you, thank you.”

“He spends a lot of time out in the shop these days. Please, come this way.” She walks briskly through the house and out the back door.

She rings a loud bell hanging from the back porch, and waves the dishtowel in the air. The farmer stops his task. She motions Jonathan over. "I'll be in the house," she smiles at him with a glad heart and reenters the back door.

As Jonathan approaches, the farmer recognizes him and staggers slightly. Jonathan glances back at the back door but decides he'd better run to his side and grab an elbow, instead.

"Are you alright, Mr. Lambert?"

"Yes, yes, It's just that, I thought I'd never see you again."

Jonathan helps him onto a stool. "Mr. Lambert, I've come to apologize for my behavior. That day you came to my house, I was having difficulties. I couldn't...," Jonathan takes a deep breath. "I wasn't ready. I behaved badly, and I'm sorry."

Mr. Lambert reflects a moment, then in a soft whisper so unlike the big husky man that he was, says, "I'm so sorry, I'm so very sorry about your little girl." He couldn't bring himself to say these words out loud. "I ask your forgiveness. I've nothing to offer you in return."

"You have it sir. And I need nothing in return. I give it freely and wholeheartedly. Please, do not carry this burden a day longer."

Jonathan enters the kitchen after Mr. Lambert. "Gina, dearest, I'm putting the kettle on. Mr. Brookes is joining us for tea. Sit, please." And he motions to a chair as Mrs. Lambert appears from the other room.

"Jonathan, please call me Jonathan, sir. 'Mr. Brookes' sounds so formal," and he grins broadly.

Mr. Lambert excuses himself to wash up and Mrs. Lambert siezes the opportunity. She takes Jonathan's hand in both of hers and in earnest says to him, "Jonathan, you coming here today, I can't tell you how much this means to my husband, to me, as well. Thank you, thank you." Her eyes dart sideways, "He just hasn't been the same since that day. It's as if," But just then Mr. Lambert reappears, and she let go of Jonathan's hand to get the kettle. Mr. Lambert helps with the cups. "On second thought, would you like to stay for supper? Lamb stew and fresh rolled bread tempting enough for you?"

"How can I refuse!" Jonathan accepts with happy anticipation.

NOBODY KNOWS

With their teacups before them, Mr. Lambert asks Jonathan, "I understand your little girl's mother, she's not with you?"

"No, sir, we never really knew her mother. Moriah was given to us, me and Henry."

"I didn't realize she had a second father. I should like to come see him someday too," says Mr. Lambert.

"I'm sorry, but he got called away on an emergency just as we arrived. He's a paramedic, in training anyway. Otherwise, he would have been here. But I must tell you something about Henry. He's taking it hard. Harder than we all thought. You see, Moriah wasn't supposed to be there when it happened." Mrs. Lambert turns from her task and sits with them at the table. Jonathan hunches over his cup, and tells them about Henry.

Mr. and Mrs. Lambert nod. But they could see Jonathan is wrestling with another, heavier burden, and so they wait in silence.

"I have not told Henry this. Not anybody. Nobody knows. Not even," He pauses, and turns his head as his eyes try to flee out the window. “Henry would not have to be taking it so hard if,” he draws a long, anguished breath, and speaks slowly,

“Henry would not have had to choose between his seat or hers, if...if had brought her home as planned in the first place.” There, he said it. He stepped through the door beyond which he only saw a dark chasm, and Jonathan knew not if there was a floor.

Mrs. Lambert rises from the table and goes to Jonathan with her arms open, and she catches him. As she holds him she says tenderly, “Let it through, just let the water through, dear.” And Mrs. Lambert held him in the circle she made with her arms until he was ready to look up again.

Jonathan returns from the washroom just as his phone rings. “It's Henry.” He looks up at them expectantly. “He's asking if it’s not too late to come over.”

Mr. Lambert looks at his wife, and they both agreed with a nod, “Perhaps Henry would like to join us tonight?” Mr. Lambert offers.

Henry arrives before supper is ready. While they wait, Mr. Lambert invites Henry to his shop to show him something he inherited from his father. Henry rises from his chair to follow Mr. Lambert. At the same time, Mrs. Lambert gently puts her hand on Jonathan's arm and implores him, “Would you mind helping an old woman with a light bulb?”

“Certainly,” he replies, and to Henry he says, “I'll be along.”

Alone with Henry at his shop, Mr. Lambert looks him in the eye and bravely asks for forgiveness, and Henry in his kindness, grants it. Henry puts his hand on Mr. Lambert's shoulders. They sit in silence for a while.

Meanwhile, as Jonathan approaches the shop, he sees through the open door, Henry with his hand on Mr. Lambert's shoulder, and Mr. Lambert sitting on a milking stool, hunched over his clasped hands. Jonathan stops, turns to go back to the farmhouse then stops again, and looks over his shoulder, then stands there a moment, deciding what to do.

THE FARMER'S SEED

“Is it alright if I ask you something about your little girl?”

“Moriah, yes, it's alright, Mr. Lambert.”

Mr. Lambert, with his head bowed, asks, “Henry, if I could ask Moriah herself, do you think she would forgive me, a complete stranger?”

“Yes, Mr. Lambert, I'm sure she would,” Henry says with conviction. He secretly wishes that he was better with words. Henry wanted so much for the old man to raise his head, so that he could see the truth in Henry's eyes. “I am certain of it. I know she would, Mr. Lambert.”

With his head still hanging down to his chest, Mr. Lambert says with much gladness, “Thank you, Henry, thank you, I hope that this will help more than I can say.”

Just then, Jonathan knocks and enters slowly. Mr. Lambert welcomes him in and motions to a barrel. Jonathan climbs on while Henry, on the bench, turns slightly to face them both.

“You both have been most gracious and kind to me, and,”

Mr. Lambert becomes very pensive, then his face lights up, and he smiles and says, “I'd like to pose a question to you, no need to answer, just a seed, for thought, if you will.”

The two young men both look at each other, then nod.

THE FUTURE

After their talk, Mr. Lambert proudly takes them to a back door leading to an extensive portion of the shop that was hidden from view. Mr. Lambert waves his hand as one would at the entrance of a kingdom that only the privileged are invited to enter. Beyond the door with broad plastic slats hanging down, they notice a second set of slats at the other side of a short foyer and beyond that, another door. On the other side was another world. The air was slightly different. There were a myriad of ferns and flowers and they realized this whole area of the building was a home to butterflies of all sorts, some they have never seen before.

Back at the farmhouse, as they start their meal, Mr. Lambert says, “My father left it to me, sadly we have no children.” Mrs. Lambert continues, “The farm, we know we shall one day sell. But the butterfly house. It pains us to think we may have to accept the reality that we will just have to leave it to total strangers.” She shakes her head and she and Mr. Lambert hold hands tightly. “We don't know the future of our butterflies.”

The boys glance at each other, then Jonathan says with wide eyes, “Mr. and Mrs. Lambert, we know someone.”

GLISTENING AND DRIPPING

Aaron contemplates whether or not it is wise to come clean with Marion before the wedding.

Aaron, looking uncomfortable in his skin, tells Marion, “I'm afraid I can't go any longer without telling you this, Marion.”

“Is this confession anything like the last one?” she gives a warning look.

“I wish it were half as funny. Recently, and more frequently, I have been having these images, I've told you, about the days surrounding Thallia's death.”

“Yes, you’ve mentioned it.”

“What I didn't tell you is,” he sighs, bracing himself for her reaction, “these flashes of images are of Mrs. Pingrey, ahem, minimally dressed.”

Aaron doesn't want to go any further but now that he has said what he has, there's no turning back.

Aaron tells her he only recalls pieces of images, his most vivid being a young Mrs. Pingrey straddling a young version of himself from behind. She is yelling something to him but he can't make out the words. Then Mrs. Pingrey's lips touching his, only her head is perpendicular to his. Then she smiles, drops of water from her hair landing on his face. Then an anxious Mrs. Pingrey looks over her shoulder towards voices, and looks at herself, scantily dressed. But before she leaves hurriedly, she says to him, "They're coming. It's going to be alright now, but they can't see me like this."

Aaron tells Marion, "I don't know which it is, Marion, dream or memory. Frankly, I'm not certain which I'd rather it be. She would probably know, but I'm too embarrassed to ask. Will you ask her for me?"

"Oh, no, Aaron, if it is what it seems to be, it would be too embarrassing for her to answer me. I couldn't do that to her. Do you think anything else happened?"

"I shudder to think so. I mean, I think of her as family, you know. It's just torture, not knowing. If something did, then with the way I've treated her all these years, as if nothing did, she must think I'm a cad or worse."

"You'll just have to face your fears. There's no way around it. You'll just have to ask her. And, I'm afraid I can't help you on this one. Ask me anything else. But, on this one, you're on your own."

Aaron asks Mrs. Pingrey out to dinner in the big city. She thought it was a bit odd. They can have a meal at any of the three different houses but he chooses a little place far away in the city to meet her. She thought, 'Perhaps he needed advice on the wedding plans.' He was already there when she arrived. After they order, she asks, "What's on your mind?"

"Well, you didn't give me much time to warm up to it. It's just as well." An angst-filled Aaron takes a long deep breath. "Have I been a cad to you all these years? If I have, I want you to know, it was never my intent to belittle what happened. All these years, me not saying anything, well, it's because I didn't remember. I don't remember. Mrs. Pingrey, Wynefred, you know I've never gotten so drunk that I don't remember, but then again if I did, then I wouldn't remember, would I? I don't know how else to ask you this, Wynefred, was I drunk that night?"

"What is this all about, Aaron?" she asks, bewildered.

"Wynefred, I swear to you on my mother's soul, I have never loved another woman after Marion. These images that haunt me. I only remember pieces. There are parts I don't remember. Have we ever...? Have you and I...please tell me...did it happen before or after the time Marion and I were married?"

"Did what happen?" she says, more perplexed.

"Wynefred, you know I have always, and will always, no matter what, have the highest regard for you. I swear it on my soul, but I need to know, did something happen between us?"

Mrs. Pingrey, finally realizes he is referring to a tryst. "Aaron, dearest, could you perhaps be mixing me up with someone else?" She says this as gently as she could, for clearly her lack of any recollection is agitating him more and more.

"Sadly, no. I have images in my head of you, your face, ahem, your lips, and more." Aaron looks like a man sentenced to death by torment. He hadn't foreseen that she, also, would not remember. "Not knowing the truth for the rest of my life would be more torturous than any man should ever bear," he confesses to her. “If I knew anything more that would help you to remember,”

Mrs. Pingrey interrupts him, her voice rising in pitch. “Not to worry, Aaron, you needn't go into any more detail. If this is some sort of pre-wedding breakdown or something, I'd like this discussion to be more helpful, and detail really wouldn't be helpful.” Mrs. Pingrey is shaking her head and starts to laugh nervously. It was very long ago that she last lost her composure in Aaron's presence, and she was trying her best to avoid it today. Moreover, she was beginning to melt from embarrassment that Aaron would have these fantasies about her when he is so close to being married to her best friend. Besides the fact that she had always thought of Aaron as family.

Aaron's dismay floods over his self-control and he exclaims, “Good grief, Wynefred, do you remember NOTHING?! I have images in my head of you, your wet shoulders glistening in the moonlight, your lips touching mine, and your hair, drenched, dripping on my face!”

Mrs. Pingrey's hand comes up to her face, she looks sideways, sees people looking their way from their own tables. “Aaron, sit, please,” she whispers, insistent.

Aaron didn't realize that he had stood up suddenly, pushing his chair backwards with a noise, and blurted out these words for all to hear. Gathering his wits about him, he announces apologetically, “Stage actors, practicing lines, so sorry, got carried away.” But as he slowly settled back down in his chair,

Mrs. Pingrey clutched the edge of the table and pushed herself away slightly. The room swirled around them, all was dark behind them. She told herself, “Breathe, Wynefred, just breathe.” As

Aaron reigned in his emotions, struggling to find words to apologize, Mrs. Pingrey's eyes once again felt comfortable meeting his. She looks at him with a smile, that surely meant the one thing he had been hoping for all this time. She has answers.

“I'm so sorry for having put you through this, Aaron. I just now realized, when you said 'moonlight,' and 'dripping.' That's when I started to put things together. Yes, something did happen long ago. We do have a special bond between us,” she says these words slowly, “but not what you think.”

IN HIGH REGARD

After some time, everyone meet at the ranch at the construction site of the newly relocated butterfly house which the Lamberts have decided to let Mrs. Pingrey take over in their stead. The family is putting up the walls. Aaron, off to one side, is behaving unusually sheepish as he works nearby.

“Well, that's a relief,” Marion declares, “a relief for everyone, don't you think?”

Mrs. Pingrey replies, “I'm just glad he blurted out those words. It was only then that I remembered. Because, if he hadn't, I wouldn't have been able to figure it out.”

“'Glistening in the moonlight,' huh? and 'dripping?'” Marion reiterates just as Aaron walks past.

Cowering behind sheetrock he is carrying, Aaron wishes he is very far away.

“It was then that I realized that he was remembering parts of the night I pulled him out of the river. I never connected the dots because I thought he was completely unconscious all that time, until just before I left. And even then,”

Aaron starts hammering the sheetrock loudly, so Mrs. Pingrey raises her voice, "even then, he was only semi-conscious. Who would think any man would remember all that he did?"

"Yes, indeed, any man." Marion yells back in reply, wondering at Aaron's odd reaction to the revelation of the heroic secret from Mrs. Pingrey's past.

"This is the best part, Marion," Mrs. Pingrey looks towards Aaron to make sure he was really listening, "He swore on his soul,"

Marion grins broadly, "Tell me, tell me."

And Aaron stops his hammering, turns to them and says, "Now, Wynefred, REALLY, is that absolutely necessary? I can take Marion knowing, but THE BOYS, TOO?" and he points his hammer to the boys working on the other wall. Aaron regrets now his choice of words the other day, 'And I've never loved another woman since Marion.'

Mrs. Pingrey had this naughty look on her face, and Aaron knew he could not hold her back now. It was too late. So he turned back to his hammering.

Mrs. Pingrey continues with much delight, "He swore on his soul that," Suddenly there was a loud thud, and a "YOWL!" as Aaron's hammer met with what sounded like flesh and bone. He dropped the hammer on the floor and cradled his injured hand. Everyone turned to him and watched helplessly as he gasped, "Hahh, hahh, water, ice, ice water, somebody, please!" Jonathan lept for the table, grabbed the cooler of ice water and unscrewed the cap for him. Henry grabbed a chair and tucked it under Aaron who fell backwards onto it just as he dunked his hand into the cooler Jonathan had opened. "Gah! Oh, mercy! It burns! It burns!"

Aaron said, as he caught his breath, “Thank you, thank you. That's much better.” He looks pitifully toward Mrs. Pingrey's now remorseful face.

“Oh, Aaron dear, I'm so sorry you were hurt,” she consoles him, as she approaches.

“He's fine, don't worry,” yells Marion, apathetically from where she stood, and turns back to her work.

“I didn't, by chance, distract you, did I?” she kneels beside him.

“Heavens, why would you think that?” he says, managing a grin through the grimace.

“Well, I was just about to say, that you swore to me on your very soul that, 'you would always hold me in high regard.' You didn't think I would say or do anything that would give you cause to change that do you? I've too much regard for you.” Then she turns to the boys. “Gentlemen, would you give us a moment, please?”

NO NEED

The boys move away and resume their work at a polite distance.

"Here," forever the nurturer, she lifts Aaron's hand above the water and lays it on his lap. "In for a few, out for a few, or you could damage cells." Then she continues, "What were you thinking?"

Aaron says with dismay, but under his breath, "I thought we agreed. There was no need to go into detail. I heard you talking to Marion." Feeling vulnerable and betrayed, he reiterates for her, "'glistening and dripping,' And then you started hollering over the noise. The boys would have heard what was next!"

"I was simply telling Marion how the droplets on the leaves glistened in the moonlight, and the water was dripping from the tops of the trees, silly, nothing more." Then she took his hand and dipped it in the ice bath once again.

Aaron's face, incredulous, "Really?"

She nods, "Most sincerely, dear."

Aaron draws a long remorseful breath, "I do apologize, Mrs. Pingrey."

"You're the one who got hurt," she says feeling awful, "I think I owe *you* an..."

He interrupts her, "Mrs. Pingrey, I should have had more faith in you." Aaron sheepishly raises his hand and shows her his thumb, cold, wet, but unharmed.

"Clever! I'm impressed. You should be a spy." A grin slid between her lips. "That's one way to stop a train." They both start laughing loudly.

Marion shouts over her shoulder, "I told you he was alright. Pulled that on me years ago. Pity his poor soul the day it really happens, no one will sympathize or come to his rescue because..."

As Marion joins the laughter, Jonathan inches over to where Henry is working, and says under his breath, "You must know she was about to reveal a juicy tidbit from his past."

Henry replies, "Yeah, he'd better mind his step, she's got something over his head."

"Do you think she'll ever tell us?" Jonathan wonders out loud.

"Nah, more leverage if she doesn't," Henry replied in his now waxing wisdom. "This is actually better than she planned." They both snicker.

Aaron, now recalls with amusement, his infamous meeting at the restaurant, which sadly, Mrs. Pingrey swears never to visit again. Mrs. Pingrey fortuitously remembered that day, and kindly obliged him all the missing pieces to his recollection of the fateful night when he almost drowned in the river long ago.

At the restaurant, Aaron chuckles, "And to think, I was going to tell Marion all that I remembered. I had rehearsed a confession in my head of what *I thought* may have happened. I'm glad I don't have to."

"Then Marion doesn't need to know everything that went through your head," she said, rescuing Aaron from his deathbed.

"Wynefred, you have rolled a great boulder off my chest," he sighed, relieved, then laughed at his own foolish assumptions.

"Believe me, it's better this way for everyone's sake. There's no need to burden *anyone's* head with images of me and my bare shoulders glistening in the moonlight, and my wet lips and hair dripping on your face." Just then a server walks past them, steps slowing. He couldn't resist a glance towards her, scanning her quickly from head to innocent toe. She caught a glimpse of him raising an eyebrow.

ON THE WING

Sometime later, Mrs. Pingrey is invited to read her poem and she invites Jonathan to read his poem, the one he wrote for her at the hospital. They approach the stage together and sit on stools near each other. Both their poems are introduced. Mrs. Pingrey reads hers with the original ending this time.

Lost But Not Forgotten followed by On the Wing of a Butterfly

....

....

....

I didn't, I couldn't, protect her you see,
It was impossible, I couldn't stand between,
This child and the hands of cruelty.
Lost but Not Forgotten, her essence, still, I seek.

I shall never have cried enough for lives that never were.
This one's essence, lost some years after birth.
If I had only known this was her fate,
I would have done anything to help her escape.

I didn't, I couldn't, protect her you see,
No possible way I could stand between
Her and the hands of her enemy,
Because I was there. Because I was she.

Mrs. Pingrey pauses then continues by introducing Jonathan, then she hands him the microphone. Then Jonathan reads his poem.

On The Wing of a Butterfly, Is What You Seek

The child who is *forever lost,* you say,
Her life's essence you think was taken away,
The child inside that you say died that day,
Is but hidden in a cocoon, it was told to wait,

For a World Anew, and the Universe Restored,
The child's essence will again be bourne,
It will emerge and come forth,
More radiant than it had ever been before.

The child is not dead or lost, you see,
The essence of lives do not so easily meet,
At mortal's hand, any sort of defeat,
Her essence lives on, that is what you seek.

It sought refuge in the chrysalis, when danger was nigh,
To grow in silence hidden beneath the sky.
Hidden from even you 'til the time was right,
To emerge, spread its wings, and then to take flight.

The answer to your question, the purpose of your life,
The reason why thrice you had not died?
You need only to seek to touch the sky,
When your wings are dry, you'll know how to fly.

Forever, the essence of that child
Shall dance on the wing of the butterfly.

Then Jonathan took her hand into his elbow and they bowed together and left the stage to join the rest of the family at their table.

That night after the poem reading in the big city, as Jonathan escorts Mrs. Pingrey to her home, she enters her doorway, turns and gives him a fond kiss, “Thank you, dear.”

“Goodnight, Mrs. P. Sleep well.”

But before she retires for the night, she visits with an old friend. Mrs. Pingrey turns on the desk lamp as she settles into her chair before her desk, and begins to pour herself out onto her trustworthy confidant. She begins to write in her notebook:

And the little girl and Pappy continued to walk along the river away from the people. Pretty soon, he lifted her up and carried her in his strong arms. She had her little arms around his neck. She was looking back behind him, where they had just come from. And she turned so she could see forward, where they were going, instead.

As rays of sunshine come through the treetops, Pappy stops walking and looks into her face.

"Are you alright?" he says softly.

She answers with a glad heart, "I am."

"Will you be alright?"

"I shall be."

"What can I do to make things better?"

At that moment, she turns into a butterfly in the hollow of his hands and he set her free to touch the sky. And she turns her gaze to look upon her world and sees that the past, present, and future are changed forever. He hears her voice on the lips of the wind, as she assures him,

"My Pappy, you already have."

With a handful of words, a heart full of compassion, and a willingness to face the danger, armed with these, as noble knights are armed with shield and sword, Pappy braved the injustice shrouded for decades in secrecy, and he rescued the little girl from an eternity of sorrow.

FOR EDMUND

The day after the poem reading, the family get together at the ranch for brunch. They had invited the Lamberts to join them, but Mrs. Pingrey explains, "Mr. and Mrs. Lambert can't come tomorrow. They would be here otherwise, and they send their best wishes. Their friend's wedding had been scheduled a long time ago. And our butterflies can't wait too much longer. They promise to be here at the next one. The butterfly house is looking good. We should be getting in more irrigation equipment in a couple of days, then we can put most of the plants on automatic. There's still lots to do, but the essentials are in."

"Well, there is one more essential," Marion motions to a box near them.

"What's in here?" Jonathan peeks in, "That's a *lot* of lights!"

Marion smiles apologetically, "Actually, there are four more boxes in the truck."

"Where did all these come from?"
"Our shed."
"Yes, but how did we get so many?"
"Hmmm, a bit of a story." She smiles.

Henry peeks in, too. “Four more! Then that would mean, gazillions!”

“Yes, I'm afraid so. I couldn't bear to part with them, sentimental, but neither have I ever had the need for all of them all at once since that first time, until now. We can put them all over the outside of the building!”

“Yup, that we can,” Aaron agrees excitedly.

“If it doesn't turn out, we can always take them down,” she offers, in case they were just humoring her.

“Oh, we'll make them turn out, alright,” Aaron reassures her. “After all, we built the butterfly house in honor of our loved ones. The lights in particular shall be in honor of Ed. That should put me on his good side, you think?” Marion smiles at Aaron adoringly.

That night, the boys and Aaron invite Mrs. Pingrey and Marion to stand outside to see the lights that they had put up all over the butterfly house in honor of Edmund. They turn off all the lights at the main house, the barn, and all around the yard, so they could see the full effect.

Henry, not wanting to take credit that wasn't theirs to claim, said excitedly, “Mother, you are marrying a genius. He engineered the whole thing!”
“Yeah,” Jonathan adds, “Aaron's brilliant!”

As everyone looks up to admire Aaron’s creative feat, Aaron looks into Marion’s face and sees the strands of stars that has descended from the heavens to light upon her eyes.

THE PROMISE

At the ranch as they enter the newly built butterfly house to prepare for the long anticipated release, Mrs. Pingrey senses a melancholy cloud hovering about the young men, "Are you gentlemen alright?"

"We were just reminiscing," says Henry.
"About the last time we made the promise," Jonathan adds.

Years ago when Moriah first came into their lives, young Jonathan and Henry made a promise to Moriah, a sacred promise they harbored in their hearts. A promise by which they lived each day since.

The day of the festival, when all the family was together, the boys asked to borrow Moriah for a while.

"We have a surprise for her. You know, like we do every year to honor her birthday."

"Even though it was two days ago, we thought renewing our promise here, now, would be more special." They grin at each other.

"You have to close your eyes, Moriah," Jonathan says to Moriah as he carries her to the foot of a large fountain nearby. When she covers her eyes, Henry reveals to the others the gossamer fairy wings he had retrieved from under the table and hid behind his back.

They both help her put on her wings and kneel before her, each taking one hand. They make the promise together, instead of separately, the way they had done in years past.

Jonathan and Henry say together:

> This is my Solemn Promise,
> Emblazoned on my Heart:
> You are My World, You are My Moriah, My Child.
> I Shall Care for You the Best Way I Can,
> I Shall Protect You With All My Might,

To their amazement, Moriah joined Jonathan and Henry in saying the last two lines.

> Until the Day I die.
> And I Promise to Love You and Honor You Forever.

Then each took her face in their hands, touched their forehead to hers, and gave her a kiss.

Whereupon she said, "I Love You, My Henry," and "I Love You, My Pappy," and gave them each a hug. And someone near them started clapping. Very soon others followed suit, and before long Moriah was surrounded by well-wishers, their beaming faces shining good thoughts their way, as the music from the Merry-Go-Round played in the distance.

Then, with her wings fluttering, Moriah ran off to where Aaron, Marion, and Mrs. Pingrey were standing, smiling, and they all waved to the boys as they continued on with the festival.

As Jonathan and Henry got up from their knees.
Henry said, "How do you think she did that?"

Jonathan replied, "You mean, 'how did she remember the last two lines?'"
Henry, still puzzled, "Yeah. It's been a whole year since the last time we said it to her."

Before he could answer, Jonathan put his hands in his pockets, and suddenly discovered something inside. "I'm such an idiot! I forgot these." And he fished out of his pocket two sparkly bracelets.

"It's alright. She won't mind if we give them to her later," Henry says reassuringly as he claps Jonathan on the shoulder.

BETTER NOW

Back again at the ranch as they enter the butterfly house, Mrs. Pingrey asks them, “Are you gentlemen alright?”

“We were just reminiscing,” says Henry.

“About the last time we made the promise,” Jonathan adds.

“Hmmm. It doesn't have to be the last, does it?” suggests Mrs. Pingrey. Then she leaves them with their thoughts, and goes to the other wing.

The young men look at each other. And smiles grow on their faces.

Henry and Jonathan enter Thallia's Wing where they keep a variety of chrysalises in various stages of development. Henry and Jonathan transfer some butterflies to a large case sitting on a cart. Suddenly, Jonathan looks up from what he is doing, and Henry does so almost at the same time.

“Do you smell that?” he asks Henry.
Henry nods.
“Are you thinking what I'm thinking?”

"Yeah."

Jonathan takes a deep breath and closes his eyes. Henry, too. They both smile, comforted by the memories stirred by the essence of Arabian jasmine, and they turn back to their work.

Before long Henry realizes something, and says, "Hey, Jonathan, I've been thinking of what you said to me on the bridge, you know..." They both now recall that day.

At the bridge near the roaring waterfall, Jonathan yells over the din, "I know what we must do."

In reply, Henry asks, "How do I do that?"

"You mean how do *we* do that?" Jonathan clarifies, then stands and pulls Henry to his feet.

Back at Thallia's Wing, "Yes, I remember," Jonathan confesses now, "Easy to say, hard to do."

"Well, I've been thinking of what Mr. Lambert asked us that one night. And I just now remembered something." Henry continues, "The day we rescued Moriah from Becka, Moriah said something to me. I didn't give it much thought then. But now, I think back..."

Henry tells Jonathan that as he carried Moriah to the main house, she whispered into his ear, "It's not Pappy's fault. It's not your fault. It's nobody's fault," she insists.

"But I feel very bad, awfully bad, just the same. Your Pappy, too, I'm sure of it," Henry confesses to her as he carries her to the breakfast bar.

Then Moriah takes his remorseful face into her hands, touches her forehead to his, and closes her eyes and sighs.

"You have felt bad long enough," Moriah consoles him, opens her eyes and then smiles, *"Do we feel better now?"*

Henry and Jonathan both smile and resume their task, now basking in their thoughts, a warm ray of sunshine in their hearts.

TIME TO LET THEM GO

After some moments, Mrs. Pingrey reenters Thallia's Wing, and wakes them from their reverie,

"Gentlemen, are you ready? *It's time to let them go."*

In front of the butterfly house, they all gather around a clear glass case filled with about a dozen different types of butterflies. Henry and Jonathan each say a few words before they both open the double doors. Most of the butterflies fly upward and outward, but one flitted around and circled the boys before flying off with the others.

The three men walk towards the main house with Aaron's arms on each of his son's shoulders. Marion joins them, but before long, Jonathan moves to the end so Aaron and Marion are together.

Jonathan looks over his shoulder toward Mrs. Pingrey who scurries to catch up to join the family, and he raises his arm and wraps it over her shoulders as they all walk and talk excitedly about wedding plans. Mrs. Pingrey turns to look back, the corners of her eyes smiling contentedly as she breathes in the melody emanating from the dancing fragments of porcelain, a homemade wind chime dangling from the eave, and beyond it on the front door hangs the big sign to the butterfly house that the family had built by their own hand.

MORIAH'S BUTTERFLY SANCTUARY

the sign says, in gold letters engraved on black stone,

and beneath the engraving hang two gold bracelets.

The End

***

ABOUT THE AUTHOR

Adalcita grew up on military bases, and has lived in many different places. She claims to have set foot on four islands in the Pacific, six different countries, and thirty-eight different states in America. That is, if you count stop-overs when she never actually left the airport, and the times she stepped out of the vehicle for gas.

She muses of someday driving an 18-wheeler truck……
even if it is just across the parking lot.

***

11517926R00133

Made in the USA
San Bernardino, CA
20 May 2014